THE MERMAID AND THE CURSED PRINCE

ALSO BY E.J. KITCHENS

*Also available as an audiobook

THE MERMAID AND THE CURSED PRINCE

E.J. KITCHENS

Brier Road Press

Songs quoted: "Head, Shoulders, Knees and Toes" (author unknown) and "Dem Bones," a spiritual song whose melody was composed by James Weldon Johnson and J. Rosamond Johnson

The Mermaid and the Cursed Prince / E.J. Kitchens —1st ed.

Paperback Print ISBN: 978-1-958167-10-6

"And she turned into sea foam . . . She deserved it for being so pathetic she couldn't even get a human prince to fall in love with her. Why does anyone like this story?"

Because they hope the same thing will happen to you and anyone else who doesn't see the actual point of the story—her devotion to the prince and refusal to harm him even to save her own life.

Lady Tala Grayrock of the merfolk kingdom of Crestfall, aged twenty-five turnings of the sea, thought it wise to bite back that unkind thought. "I don't think that is the point of the story, Princess Meilani," was all she said. *In truth,* she added to herself, *if you think about how impulsively she disregarded her home and sacrificed so much for a prince she didn't even know, demanding he marry her, her devotion turns into something not so admirable. But some stories aren't meant to be parsed to that level.*

Or turned into failed flirter stories.

Hoping that reply was sufficient, Tala continued engraving decorative designs into the turtle shell she'd found and inscribed with a story from her people she thought her human friend—Princess Liliana of Birney—would enjoy.

Meilani flapped her tail fins in irritation but remained near the bronze mirror, wedged between rocks, that Tala had found in an old wreck when she was young. The sixteen-year-old princess, her cousin, fluffed her lavender hair, a lighter shade than her scales, and watched as it floated down to her shoulders in graceful waves. "If I ever took a fancy to a human prince, I would certainly win his heart." Meilani flung herself away from the mirror to hover over Tala's shoulder, causing the water, warmed by a natural vent, to brush against Tala's skin in a staccato rhythm.

Heart pounding, Tala barely kept her place by the desk-like rock ledge and her hand from her stone dagger. A sudden movement of water often meant an impending attack —the polite pace of approach did not cause the warning pulse. Twitching her own fins to let out the tension unobtrusively, she went back to engraving and let Meilani study the shell.

Tala did not normally mind visitors to her little grotto in a rarely used part of the sea kingdom of Crestfall. She enjoyed sharing its beauties—elegant sea anemones with gently waving tentacles, shelves of brightly colored shells and intriguing human trinkets she'd found. Or that her friends had given her during her visits to the human kingdom of Birney with her ambassador uncle. She even had a few squid pets that provided a pleasant greenish light.

There were, however, a few exceptions to her desire for visitors, and one of those was a particular princess. Nonetheless, Tala forced a smile and pointed out her favorite of the turtle shell's decorations: a stylized sun sinking into the water beside a forested cliff. Meilani at least appreciated her art, if nothing else.

"You may not hold with lying," Meilani said imperiously

after a genuine compliment of her work, "but you are very good at it."

The shark-tooth stylus stuck in the shell. *I beg your pardon!*

"This human princess, she believes you are her friend." Meilani swam away to a squid's perch and began idly examining her collection of bracelets in its light. "I heard she's cursed. I want to know all about it. You'll visit her with your uncle next week and speak with her. She is much more likely to tell you—a siren and her supposed friend—all the things that the king would not tell an ambassador."

"I did *not* inherit my great-grandmother's siren gift, as it doesn't continue in mixed blood, and why are you even interested? You think humans are boring." *And Lily is my friend!* Tala did not ask why she *should*. The answer with Meilani was always to avoid some sort of punishment. From the way the princess was looking around her treasured alcove, it would be the loss of her prized hideaway.

"Yes," agreed a masculine voice from behind them. Malosi, thirty turnings of the sea, lounged on a rock near the vent of heated water. He was Meilani's cousin (on the other side) and was an ambassador to the human kingdom of Litvania, the very large bully of a kingdom that backed the peninsular Birney, and which often tried to swallow it. "You've called them boring and colorless multiple times, cousin." He smiled, showing off his sharpened teeth, something some merfolk did to align themselves with strong predators. It did not help the uncomfortable feeling he and Litvania were well suited to one another. "After all, little Birney only has one prince, and he is already engaged, so you couldn't try your charming skills on him."

"I could still have the human prince if I wanted," Meilani protested, her hands going to her scaled hips. "*That* would make humans interesting."

The merman laughed derisively, and Meilani's face took on a stubborn look Tala did not like.

"You could not even convince Lady Octavia to make you human, little one. *If* you could find her. And you could never find a fae in the ocean, or one of their artifacts."

Tala shot Malosi a look. He was hardly helping matters. "Birney's Prince Lysander is quite happily matched. It would be difficult to sway him and dishonorable to try." Not to mention his betrothed's father had insisted on a marriage agreement that would cripple Birney and start a war if breached. "And you have said yourself you do not like the human world, and that legs are ugly, so it really does not matter. Tell me about this merprince of Vanu Sami you met recently. Is he not still sending you pearls every week?"

Meilani huffed even as she touched a strand of choice pearls about her waist. "Is that not my point? Would not a merprince be harder to charm than a human one? The mermaid in the story was incompetent."

"Undoubtedly. It wouldn't be much of a triumph where most of them are concerned." *Not with your exotic looks and confidence.*

Malosi, inspecting a couple of numbered die Birney's king had given her, chuckled. "So cynical, Tala. You used to be so enamored of the human world . . . that is, until they killed your parents. Such a pity, drunken sailors crashing their boat on a reef and pieces of the boat catching your parents on their way back from that little kingdom your uncle still bothers to try to keep independent. You rarely visit anymore, I'm told."

Turning back to her work to cover a hard swallow, Tala finished engraving a wave before replying. "I am not so foolish as to blame humans in general. They are surprisingly like us—there are decent ones and bad ones, and some who swing swiftly from one to the other. It's simply a long trip to Birney, and though I love the people, it's not very comfortable there." If she ever found the man who came up with those contraptions . . .

Malosi threw his head back in laughter. "I imagine it is rather uncomfortable. The king of Litvania comes down to *me*."

Tala rolled her eyes and continued working.

"*I* don't think the contraption would be so terrible," Meilani said in a whiny tone. "I would like to see the human world up in the castle itself, not just in a cave grotto."

"I don't think so, Mei," Malosi said in a condescending tone. "It's cold and dry up in the human dwellings. They don't have warm water to surround them, and air doesn't hold warmth as water does. They have fires, which while enchanting to watch create a smelly fog called smoke that dries out your skin and makes you cough." He paused to run his fingers through his long ebony hair. "And of course, as an exotic mermaid, everyone would be staring at you."

Meilani tossed her hair over her shoulder, making it and her scales shimmer. *Oh, she likes to be stared at.*

With iridescent lavender scales reaching from the tip of her fins to what human Princess Lily called a "sweetheart neckline," silky lavender hair, a full figure, and a confidence to match, Meilani would make even the most stodgy of men —human or merman—look twice, or thrice. Tala's scales were a more common sapphire blue with a hint of iridescence, her hair an unremarkable chestnut brown, and men often looked twice at her. She could only imagine Meilani's reception.

Clothes would help with the cold, but you'd be vulnerable, unable to escape since you can't walk. The contraptions are hard to maneuver and basically trap you inside. Tala shivered at that unwelcome feeling, which was soothed only by trust in Birney's royal family and the loyalty of their guards.

"The contraption would hide your beautiful scales,

Princess Meilani," Tala countered with a point of vanity that might work on her younger cousin.

"Have *you* ever seen a fire?" the princess challenged Malosi instead.

"Yes, and without a contraption."

With a gasp, Meilani swam through the water to curl up on the rock beside him. "How?"

"That is my secret, squirt," Malosi replied with a smug smile that unsettled Tala. For once she wished Meilani would wheedle information from someone.

Instead, the princess huffed and moved away toward the narrow opening between the boulders that made the grotto safe from any large predators that breached the defenses of the sea canyon in which her kingdom stood.

"Don't forget, Tala, that I want to know all about the human's curse—and any princes who come to save her from it." With a goodbye, Meilani swiftly disappeared into the blue depths.

"Should I go after her and talk sense to her?" Malosi asked lazily from his warm perch.

You are always welcome to leave.

"I don't believe sense is something Meilani has learned to value yet, but you are welcome to attempt it."

With a deep, pleasant-sounding laugh, Malosi pushed away from the rock. It was a pity his character didn't match his looks and voice. "You could be a great ambassador if you would choose to be. And if you used your siren heritage."

There was an intensity to his look as he paused beside her that unnerved her.

"I have no desire for a political life," she said as she hunched over the shell, "and I did not inherit the siren gift to use even *if* it was legal."

"Legal for ordinary and for the king's servants aren't always the same." At her offended gasp, he smiled, showing off his shark-like teeth, wished her a good day, and left.

From the dull rumbles floating through the water a moment later, he'd caught up with Meilani and was talking to her. Tala felt a twinge of worry. It was unlikely Meilani would remain interested in the scheme for long, or use the details of Lily's curse against them, but still Tala couldn't help but pray a curse was all the trouble her human friend had to face.

She was happily working again when the gentle brush of water against her arms announced another set of visitors—her aunt and uncle. Among the merfolk, siblings often lived together, so she'd been close to them even before the death of her parents made them her guardians. With silver streaks in their hair and edging their turquoise tails, they were as lovely as they were kind.

"*Ia mafanafana pea le vai,*" she greeted them happily as her aunt swam over to kiss her cheek. *May the water always be warm.*

"*Ma fa'amama ou aso uma.*" *And clear all your days.* Aunt Tiare finger-combed Tala's chestnut hair in a soothing pattern as she admired her work.

"Were Malosi and Princess Meilani coming from here?" Uncle Fetu asked, tone almost wary, as he settled by the warm vent.

"Yes."

"Malosi's been about more than usual lately, hasn't he?"

"I suppose so." Tala, happy to have exchanged tiresome visitors for some of her favorites in all the world, turned contentedly back to her art, humming as she worked.

Had she looked up then, and seen the frown on her uncle's face and the worried look exchanged between him and her aunt, her life might have turned out quite different.

CHAPTER 2

on't drown. Don't drown.

D Prince Rowan of the Kingdom of Danskov rued every former time he'd failed to ask directions. That was not an option now even if he could currently speak. He'd seen no sign of the island all day, and he was beginning to feel the shrinking already starting. Just a twinge but beginning. What cove was deep enough with a safe shore—and near? If he didn't find one soon, his night as a human would be his last ever. Blast curses! And blast kings who thought marrying conniving fairy godmothers was the only way to save their little kingdoms from their larger neighbors.

Sighing, Rowan pushed himself faster through the water, all his senses alert for an island.

Of course, if he ever did find Lady Octavia, there was no telling what would happen. Or if he was being even more foolish than his father.

CHAPTER 3

"And she turned into sea foam! Just goes to show you how trying to force someone into doing what you want ends up." Curled up comfortably on her enormous bed—such a soft, warm-looking thing!—Princess Liliana of Birney finally lay the turtle shell aside. She traced her finger over the edging work again, a strange smile on her lips.

But then, everything about her face looked strange now.

Tala hid a shiver as she turned back to the view out the princess's window, across the balcony, and over the city and sea. She could smell the sea here, and it was a comfort in the dry air on her face and arms, as she'd been ashore in the detested contraption since the morning. Early after its conception—by some foreign prince who fancied himself an inventor—an attachment had been added to the contraption to hold a jar with sea water and a rag, should she need it, and she reached for it now.

"What does Princess Meilani want to know about my curse?" Lily asked.

"Are you sure you should tell me?" Tala paused in bathing her arm to watch water drip down her skin, from her elbow to her hand. To see water drip was a strange thing! She was used to being a part of it, not a separate thing. She looked up at Lily again, as her uncle had stressed how important eye contact was for Lily, more so than for other humans, though he'd never given a reason. "As your friend, I want to know all you choose to tell me, but if my princess asks . . . "

Lily made a *ftt* sound and waved the question away. "What can a mermaid princess do to me? The pertinent details were spread about by the mage who cursed me anyway: Princess becomes hideously ugly. Young man— preferably a prince—must rescue princess from Golden Tower and defeat the magical bull in the courtyard. Bull will then turn into a large, fiery bird. Young man must get bird to lay an egg. Said egg, which will be aflame, must not be allowed to break or touch the ground, lest it set things on fire. Young man must present egg to mage.

"Winner is supposed to get me, naturally. We think someone paid that horrid sorcerer Crystim to do it, just don't know why." Lily sighed heavily and slumped against her pillow. "We've had a deluge of princes and nobles hoping to rescue me from the Golden Tower. Most have gotten hurt and been carried home. Grandfather is about to forbid anyone from trying for a time."

How long will you have to stay cursed? What if you don't like the prince who gets the egg? Why would anyone pay a mage to curse you? "But you're not in the Tower. Isn't that in the mountains, near the Litvanian border?"

"Of course not, and yes, it is. We're always getting stuck in the Tower for some curse or other, so we keep it nicely stocked with supplies and an escape hatch. I waited a day and then walked out."

"I wonder how the mage felt about that."

Lily shrugged and was silent a moment, during which Tala played with the water, dribbling it down her arm. It was a convenient excuse to not look at her friend.

"And you don't squirm and run away when you see me," Lily continued, finally sounding as glum as Tala would be in a similar state.

Tala did look up then. "It's not without effort, I assure you. I won't insult your curse by denying it."

Lily laughed, and that made even the contraption worth it. Even if the laugh gave her shivers. "We don't dare risk that." Lily's expression turned unusually thoughtful, and the Tala of five years ago would have teased her about a beau if she'd seen that look, but the twenty-five-year-old Tala merely returned a sad smile of acknowledgement.

It was, unfortunately, a common occurrence for members of the royal family of the little seaside kingdom to suffer from misadventures of a magical kind. Lily's curse by a malicious mage had left her skin gray, her eyes hideously large, her teeth bucked, her laugh cringe-inducing, and her red hair somehow reminiscent of the color of that remaining on the long-dead sailors Tala had once seen exploring a shipwreck.

"It sometimes takes a storm to stir the sea and reveal treasure," Tala recited a proverb her aunt repeated whenever she was annoyed or upset by troubles.

"I'll take that one on a shell too." Lily mused a few minutes, then with a groan, sat up and swung her legs over the edge of the bed. "It's time to join my grandfather and your uncle for their meeting. I tried to get us out of it, but they insisted. Those two are up to something. I can see it in their eyes. Shall I escort you or will you handle it yourself?"

"I'll manage." Teeth gritted, Tala adjusted the enormous skirt of the cream-colored gown hiding the bell-shaped tank-on-wheels that allowed her to visit the castle proper. To think when she'd been a little mermaid excited to visit the human world with her uncle, she'd been grateful for these ridiculous contraptions. She reached through the layers of tulle to grasp the cranks that allowed her to direct the tank. Flipping her fins to provide the force, she used the left and right cranks to guide the wheeled contraption away from her window-facing vantage point to the door. By some miracle, the thing moved—squeak by squeak.

How sorely she missed meeting in the grotto under the castle! King Basil was now too frail for the descent.

"Still want to make the inventor walk a plank?" Lily asked as she held the door open.

"If I had siren powers, *yes*. I would gleefully talk him into it."

"Well, it may feel like a fish tank on wheels, but you look stunning," Lily said as she followed her out. "I'm sorry about the noise. I guess they missed a spot when they oiled the thingamabobs for you."

"Next time, please make sure they oil all the thingam-abobs." *Whatever those are. Some part of the wheels or axles maybe?*

"I will," Lily said, something suspiciously mischievous in the tilt of her lips and the glint of her eye.

"What?"

"Nothing. Nothing." Lily twirled a sickly red curl self-consciously for a few paces down the hallway before asking, "What do you think of Prince Maximilian? The young man you met when you arrived? The one with the light-brown hair and lanky build? Not classically handsome, but a friendly, kind sort of face one quickly gets used to? When he saw me, he didn't cringe and he didn't run away." Finally stopping to draw breath, she frowned. "He didn't go into a corner and throw up either. Now *that* was embarrassing. That prince didn't even try to get to the Tower." The frown brightened into a smile Tala hoped Lily wasn't smitten enough to give this Prince Maxim-ilian yet. "Max just said, 'Wow, what did you do to earn that curse?' It was the nicest thing anyone ever said to me."

"What did you say?"

"I was born in Birney."

Tala laughed and was about to ask if Max, an exiled prince who'd sought sanctuary with them, was interested in going to the Tower, but more squeaking announced her uncle and his guards also nearing the meeting room. The fierce mermen looked like they were standing in tin cans painted to look like fancy trouser legs against a seashore with crabs scurrying across the sand. The crabs had noticeable eye stalks and were watching them. One was winking. One guard's contraption had an octopus being squished underfoot, its eyes bulging and arms failing comically. Such an indignity for a relative of the king of the greatest underwater kingdom! Such an indignity for even guards, for any merman! If she ever found that inventor . . .

A sly twinkle lit her uncle's eye before he smiled at her and Lily. One of the castle cats, as usual, was comfortably curled up in his arms. "There you are, dears. I must say I've been looking forward to this."

King Basil and Prince Lysander greeted them as well, and Tala put thoughts of revenge aside. They soon settled in for reports on the sea-going vessels her kingdom had protected from sirens or playful orcas or helped salvage, and so on. With the sound of waves splashing in the background, her uncle beside her, familiar topics discussed, she could almost forget the knot in her stomach drawing her to the safety, beauty, and freedom of the sea—out of that horrid contraption.

As the meeting drew to a close, her uncle and the king exchanged a look that reminded Tala of Lily's prediction.

"We have exciting news," King Basil declared, his voice firm despite his difficultly walking. "With both sadness and joy, King Aleki of Crestfall and I accept my dear friend Fetu's retirement as ambassador and the appointment of his replacement, who is already beloved by us."

Tala's gaze shot to her uncle. He'd been speaking of

retiring for years but had always seemed to enjoy his work despite the effort. Why hadn't he told her?

He looked oddly peaceful, that worried look about him she'd begun to notice the past week gone.

She was glad he was at peace with the decision, but who could possibly replace him that Birney's royal family already knew? They'd met Malosi, but surely her uncle wouldn't let their king appoint hi—

"To Lady Tala, our new ambassador to Crestfall!" King Basil raised a glass in toast, and Tala's jaw dropped. "And per the king's and your uncle's suggestion, you're to be our guest for the next month to help our people better understand one another."

The contraption squeaked as Tala's tail fins twitched in anxiety, but she smiled at the old king, his heir, her uncle, and her friend, hoping just this once she was as good a liar as Meilani claimed.

CHAPTER 4

Tala had survived three weeks in the human world. Surely she could survive another?

There's been an unusual amount of shark activity in the water recently. It wouldn't be safe to swim home anyway.

"King Basil thinks it's important for you to see an inland lake and how the river feeding it flows to the sea. A lot of commerce comes through the ports here because of the rivers." Twenty-two-year-old Prince Maximilian of Danskov briefly raised his ever-present floppy brown cap to scratch his head as he studied the barrel of sea water loaded into a horse-drawn cart. Tala suspected there was something magical about the cap, but Max, as he'd swiftly come to be known, wouldn't answer any questions about it or how he and his brothers had come to be exiled while on good terms with their father.

"No." Tala, currently lounging in the courtyard fountain while Lily sat on the edge and read, crossed her arms and gave him a flat look. "Absolutely not."

Beside her, Lily chuckled and hid her face in the book when Tala glared at her. There no heat to the glare though, and little mirth in the chuckle. A prince had died in his quest to the Golden Tower a few days before, and King Basil had forbidden any more attempts. Lily had taken the former very hard. Tala wasn't exactly sure about the latter, not from the way Lily and Max looked at one another. Which was quite a feat given how Lily looked. The family did have a magic mirror that let others see her true form, and King Basil had made a point of letting Max see her the second week after his arrival. The pair could spend hours just talking, Max watching Lily in the mirror, smiling when she smiled, and sometimes just smiling at her, forgetting to even answer. Yet he could also look at her the same way without the mirror's aid.

"Then how are we going to get you there?" Max rubbed his hair again, an amusingly perplexed look on his face. *I hope you rescue Lily so I can have you as a kid brother.* "King Basil appointed me as head of the expedition. We've got to go."

"Then use your head to figure it out."

When he shot her a look and pulled the cap down over his unruly hair with a purposeful tug, Tala grinned at him in challenge.

"You know they wrap fish in newspaper in the markets, don't you?"

Tala drew back. "I am not a fish."

"Coulda fooled me, Fins."

As Tala splashed water at Max, Lily said, only half jesting, "You could wrap her in a wet blanket. She acts like one sometimes. Horseback would be faster too. You could carry her."

"Me?" Max cried, his eyes going wide. "But the blanket would be wet, and she'd be sitting in my lap."

"Yes."

"That would make the front of my pants wet."

"Is there something wrong with that?" Tala asked innocently as Max's eyes grew wider and Lily bit back a smile. "You humans have such an odd relationship with water. You live by and drink it and love to watch it flow, but you fear being touched by it!"

Max looked between the two girls, something more keen than embarrassed in his expression. He sighed dramatically. "No. Wet blanket and horseback it is then."

This time it was Tala's time for wide eyes. She really ought to be more careful with her teasing.

Not sure if she won or lost that challenge, Tala was soon wrapped in sea-water soaked blankets and riding in a foreign prince's lap on a horse along a coastal road. Additional water was carried in the saddle bags—she'd made sure of it. Lily, veiled as she always was in public, rode beside them and a few guards behind. Prince Lysander was away in Litvania for a diplomatic meeting and so wasn't with them for this outing.

They were rather worried about him, as Litvania was attempting to force Birney and the kingdom of Lysander's bride to allow them to host the upcoming wedding as a show of support for the union. The situation with Phoebe's kingdom was already rocky enough, and both were wary of grasping Litvania, hence the marriage alliance. Tala was exceptionally grateful Meilani hadn't shown up here to toy with Lysander. Perhaps she had a new interest besides the human world, or she couldn't find Lady Octavia to bespell her into a human form, but either way, Tala was thankful.

"You could have put an oil blanket down on your lap," Tala said quietly to Max an hour into their ride, as they started to turn back to the shore before going up into the mountains. Max had been staring toward the mountain with the Golden Tower with an unusually serious expression for some time. He only looked away to watch the eagle she often spotted following them. She had an odd feeling she'd seen the creature around the castle too. And the blue whale splashing off the shore.

She cocked an eyebrow at him, and he grinned sheepishly as he looked down at her.

"I know, but your and Princess Lily's laughter was worth it."

Just as I thought. "You're a good man, Max."

Blushing, he tugged his cap down. "Thank you, Sushi."

"You're not going to do anything rash, are you?" She jerked her chin toward the tree-covered mountain hiding the Golden Tower from view, and his jaw clamped.

"No . . . I guess not. I . . . " He glanced at Lily, then at the eagle and whale, expression torn, then tugged his hat down. When he spoke again, it was with a playful tone. "You know people would get the wrong idea if they saw us riding like this."

"I can't imagine why," Tala said drily as she smoothed down the skirts hiding her blankets and fins. "I'm quite competent riding the large sea horses, you know. I wish I could show them to you! After riding *that*, I wouldn't want anyone to think I couldn't handle a *land* horse." She looked up at a whiff of sea air and watched waves lap the shoreline below.

"I have a big brother you know," Max continued, apparently determined for mischief. "Two actually, but you only need one, and I think I know the one."

"Does he have fins?" She leaned forward as something uncharacteristically colorful broke the water. It was almost the particular emerald color of scales common to her people.

"Well . . . he does spend a lot of time at sea . . . I'm hoping to hear good news about that soon." His voice dropped to a whisper, "Because if it's not good news, it will be very bad news."

"No offense, but I like fins. Turquoise scales preferably." Was that a long strip of emerald fabric in the waves, with a bit of red on it? From a shipwreck perhaps? No merfolk would flop like that. She leaned out a little further, and Max's arm about her waist tightened to compensate.

"Fins? You mean shark fins? I hear they're tasty."

"Max, stop it!" Lily squealed. "She wants a handsome *merman*."

"But my brother's not a merman."

"Max, stop! Stop the horse!" Tala grabbed his arm and gestured to the sea. "There's a merman near the shore." And he was floating aimlessly in the water rather than swimming powerfully through it—he was hurt, or worse.

⚓

The guards riding ahead, they found a road down to the shore and galloped across the sand until they reached the spot where Tala had seen the emerald and red. When Max drew their horse to a slow walk near it, the guards were already wading into the water toward an unconscious merman. Though bleeding, he still clutched a spear. She vaguely recognized him as a Crestfall guard, one recently sent to Litvania with Malosi. What had happened?

"Max, throw me in." She was already wiggling toward the edge of his lap, and he directed the horse into the water and lowered her in. She slipped out of the dress and blankets and swam for the merman just as the two guards reached him. They released him to her, and she pulled him out into the deeper water and checked his wounds. He had a pulse, thank heavens! A shark bite on his lower tail was responsible for some of the bleeding. Her brows furrowed. The wound on his side did not look like any sea creature sting or bite she had seen. The entry hole was . . . more like a knife wound.

Tala put that especially troubling thought aside for later and began towing the heavy merman back to shore.

She couldn't get him home with sharks prowling the

waters. They would be too vulnerable, and any scent of blood from his wounds . . . No, even if her escort were here, it would be too risky. The humans would have to treat him. He'd do better underwater though. Perhaps he could stay in the fountain or—

"Lady Tala." The guard's words were weak, but they gave her hope he'd live.

She patted his chest in acknowledgement but continued to swim for shore. "Quiet now. I'll get help. The humans will help you."

"It's your humans in danger, and our king," he said haltingly, and Tala froze. "Malosi has allied with Litvania and the siren kingdom . . . He's promised Birney to Litvania and promised Litvania . . . that all the sea people would cause destruction to the vessels of other kingdoms passing through their waters." As the coldness of horror swept down Tala's body, the guard struggled to keep speaking. "Princess Meilani," he managed to get out at last, "has come to Litvania —as a human. She cannot speak, but she is trying to woo Prince Lysander. She will fail, and as Malosi has some hold on the curse or the sorcerer who gave it, he will hold her fate as ransom, for she will turn into sea foam the morning after Prince Lysander marries. To save his daughter, our King Aleki will give up his kingdom. You must get word to him. He mustn't give Malosi our people."

CHAPTER 5

"Well, look what the cat dragged in."

"I see I'm not your only guest, Lady Octavia," an unfamiliar man—a mage of some kind—said.

Rowan, gasping for breath, crawled another few feet toward the shore, water lapping against his back. *If you stay here, you're going to be a beached whale by morning. Find strength somewhere!*

But his body didn't want to comply with his orders to stand. The transformation from whale to human had taken him miles from shore, and he'd had to swim the rest of the way—and swimming had never been his strong suit. *Get up!*

The pair watching from the shore were no help, but he wasn't being magically dragged under, so perhaps Lady Octavia wasn't going to kill him on sight. No one knew how old she was—or dared to guess. Magi—the enchanters allied with Mage Isle and the mostly criminal sorcerers who refused to live by their ethics—lived a very, very long time. Whether by age or choice or nature, she had a cascade of frizzy white hair that fell over broad shoulders and a shapeless dress—belted and bearing a curved sword. He had a feeling she could be decently attractive in a powerful, larger-built way, but she didn't know how. Consequently, she just looked powerful, dangerous, and a bit sour. Some desperate part of him hoped that last bit was a ruse.

He paused his crawling to raise a hand in greeting. "Well met, Aunt!"

The formidable woman's face pinched. *Not good.*

"Is that one of your sister's fairy godchildren, perchance?" the mage asked the woman on whose island he stood. He was a thin, dark-haired man, sort of a stereotype dapper villain. Neat, dark clothes, hair slicked back, a cloak that flapped ominously behind him despite the stillness of the air. He even had what Rowan guessed was a sword stick. "Er, stepchildren now, if rumors of a certain semi-forbidden human-enchantress marriage are correct?"

"I don't claim any children—godchildren, regular children, or nieces and nephews," was the terse reply.

Rowan winced. *Then perhaps you're at least interested in spiting your sister?*

When he tried to stand but couldn't, he threw pride to the wind and kept crawling through sand and waves until he was a half-dozen feet from the magi. "I do hope I'm not intruding."

Lady Octavia huffed. "Get up or I'll have the crabs drag you out to the sharks. I won't have a human expiring and decomposing on my shore."

"It's not a future that inspires me either, dear Aunt." The threat *did* inspire him into staggering to his feet. The waves lapping at his legs nearly toppled him, but he managed to take the necessary steps forward to get beyond their reach. Feeling a bit steadier on the rock walkway, he followed Lady Octavia and her guest to the mansion taking up most of the little island found only by magic or by those touched by magic—or those cursed, as he was.

As he crossed the threshold a blast of air hit him, and he

had to grab the doorframe to keep his feet underneath him, but when it stopped, he was dry. "Thank you, Aunt. I feel much better now—and I won't leave any unsightly stains on your furniture."

She huffed and, after leading them to a sitting room, gestured him to a chair near the fire, then pointed to her companion. "This is Crystim, a mercenary enchanter. Crystim, Prince Rowan of Danskov."

Crystim gave a proud bow. "If you ever desire a curse upon an enemy, Your Highness, or dare I say, even a kingdom toppled, I would be honored to aid you. For a fee of course."

"Of course. Are you working on anything currently?" Rowan asked in an innocent tone as he brushed a hand through his wild, damp hair. A servant fetched him a glass of wine, and Rowan noted the tray of crackers, cheese, and barely touched glasses between his aunt's chair and the mage's.

Surely it would be too much of a coincidence for this mage to be the one hired to harass the princess his little brother was fond of? But then, Birney wasn't that far away.

Neither was Litvania.

That was a fate all Litvania's neighbors lamented. Both Birney and Danskov shared a border with it, though they themselves were a good distance apart. Danskov was mountainous, yet it boasted some ports of its own, which Litvania wanted. A few years prior, Rowan's father, after learning that their much, much larger neighbor had plans to invade them, had, in desperation, asked his children's fairy godmother for help. She suggested a marriage alliance. Seeing no better option, his father agreed. She threatened Litvania's royal family, and they'd been safe ever since—at least from conquering kingdoms. His stepmother had hung around a good deal more than the marriage of convenience warranted, and when his father began contemplating turning over the kingdom to his oldest son, things had swiftly changed. And so had they.

"You must be exceptionally talented and sought after to be involved in matters of kingdoms," Rowan said with completely insincere awe. "You wouldn't mind sharing your portfolio, would you?"

The mage practically preened at the invitation. "Well, I shouldn't say, but since your stepmother and aunt are so well thought of, I know you're safe to confide in, and as you say, it is *my* portfolio . . . " He leaned forward, and when Rowan matched his posture, he said in a lowered voice, "Litvania and the merfolk kingdom of Crestfall are current clients of mine. Well, that is to say, a representative of Crestfall asked me to secure the kingdoms of Birney and Crestfall, and the siren city, for him and Litvania."

Rowan didn't need to feign shock at that. The merfolk were involved! "What a tremendous task!" he blathered to keep the man talking.

Crystim shrugged modestly. "It would have been impossible for many, I'm sure, but with the power of my crystal ball . . . " He sighed contentedly and reclined in his seat. "It's all in motion now, and I am here with your gracious aunt, awaiting the curses' end. Of course, the terms will never be met by those cursed, but I am bound to remain nearby, in case. The hope of an end, you know, is a sure driver in these cases. Very useful."

In other words, the mage was hiding because he'd sunk too much power into the curses and was vulnerable until that power was regained at the spells' end.

You had better not walk too close to the shore tomorrow, mage, or you may find out what it's like to be swallowed by whale.

"That is brilliant!" Rowan exclaimed with a small clap. "I will keep your services in mind."

After a few minutes of small talk, the mage excused himself for the evening, and Rowan wondered if information-gathering and blackmail were also part of the mage's portfolio.

"I would recommend stargazing on the lower terrace," Lady Octavia said cooly as the man bowed to them.

Crystim laughed uncomfortably and seemed about to say something, but at a dark look from Lady Octavia, he bowed again. "I look forward to the beauty of your skies, Lady Octavia."

"I'll have my servants help you with the mounted telescope."

The inner doorway opened, and her butler appeared, his gaze landing expectantly on the mage. Crystim cleared his throat and left, wishing them a good night.

As the door closed behind him, a heavy silence fell on the room, and Rowan grinned brightly at the woman who'd often been trapped into fulfilling her sister's godmother duties for three rambunctious, motherless princes. He'd seen her but little in the last three years, during which time his stepmother had been generous with rumors about her.

Lady Octavia huffed again, but a spark of something lit her eye, giving Rowan hope the idea he'd formed of her as a boy was more accurate than the one he'd heard as a man—the story of a rogue enchantress feared by her fellow magi, humans, and merfolk alike. Who'd sailed the seas in the days of the sirens' and kracken's rule, and who'd single-handedly, ruthlessly brought their terror to an end. And though that had brought safety to the merfolk, even they feared her. *I don't know how you did that, but I hope you still have a soft spot for wild boys with a tendency to jump out of trees on unsuspecting visitors.*

Lady Octavia continued to watch him from over the rim of her wine glass until the men's footsteps disappeared into the gentle crashing of waves. In the stillness that followed, she set down the glass. "Now, nephew, why are you here? I doubt my sister sent you."

"She didn't. Your sister decided to take it upon herself to —how shall we say it?—cure my brothers and me of our fears."

One incongruously dark eyebrow arched. "You fear drowning."

"I got over that when I was ten," he said in fake irritation to cover the start that she remembered. "But be that as it may, I am now a whale by day."

He said no more, and her lips pinched. *Come on, you know us. You just proved you do.*

"Beau is afraid of heights," she said at last, and he almost cheered.

"He is an eagle by day. And Max . . . " He took another sip of wine, watching her watching him.

She narrowed her eyes at him, but when he stuck to his silence, she sighed and finished for him. "And Max had a bad dream when he was seven that all his family died, then he lost his mother. He's been afraid of the rest of you leaving him ever since."

Barely keeping himself from smiling, Rowan nodded. "After Beau and I were 'treated,' he snuck away to get help and avoid a similar bitter medicine. A few hours later she exiled him. He ended up in Birney, hoping to get help from the family's fairy godparents. Turns out their princess is cursed too."

What the curse and cure for Princess Lily were, Max had never specified. *It's an unfortunate curse. But some folk look that way naturally*, was all his brother had said about it.

"I see. And you want me, from some supposed affection for three human brats, to uncurse you?"

"No, I want you to uncurse us to spite your sister."

Lady Octavia's eyebrows rose, and then she threw her head back and laughed. Something in Rowan's chest loosened. He'd always found those rare laughs more inviting than her sister's elegant ones, and he'd always wanted to encourage more of them.

"If I were to ever like any humans," she said as she quieted, her sourness vanishing, "it would be you boys. But as I think you know, my sister is too clever for me to simply report her to Mage Isle for you, even if they would listen to me. She would plead that she was trying to help you overcome your fears and didn't understand how stressed it would make you. Her spells are tricky too, so it would be no simple matter to uncurse you."

Rowan's heart sank, but he'd been struggling to stay afloat too long to give up now. *Please.*

"What I *can* do, however," she continued, "is spite both her and the simpering mercenary mage who invited himself to my sanctuary to cower." A very alarming grin reminded him of her reputation as dangerous. "I believe the terms of the Birney princess's curse involve collecting an egg." Rowan had no idea but nodded. Why hadn't his brother done something about it if he was so besotted with the girl? "Within the egg is a crystal ball. It is in large part the source of Crystim's magic. That's uncommon and not very wise on his part to have put his magic in it. The one who holds the crystal ball could not only remove the curse on the princess but would gain its power, gain wishes, you might say. So the one who holds the crystal ball could feasibly threaten other kingdoms with its power. How much power it has, I don't know. I wouldn't waste wishes before using it on yourself."

Rowan sank back in his seat and let out a heavy breath. That wasn't what he was expecting, though he'd not known what to expect, to be honest. *Free the Danskov family of its curses* was only one wish—that was all he and Beau needed. So all he needed to do was go on a quest for an egg.

During his few hours as a human at night.

All Max and Beau needed to do was hunt an egg. While he swam aimlessly.

"I see," Rowan said, reminding himself he'd gotten the information. He didn't have to do everything to free himself and Beau, his father and kingdom, from his stepmother.

"Yes, I'm glad you do," Lady Octavia said as she relaxed into her chair as well, a slight smile on her lips. "I need you gone by morning of course. I won't have a decaying whale on my shoreline either—or one bursting my home. And see that you don't spend all your nights here."

"Yes, my lady," Rowan said, trying not to smile. "Oh, I was wondering if I might try tinkering together a boat while I'm here, if you have any spare parts lying around? It would be comforting not to fear not making landfall by curse's end each day."

"There might be some. You can talk to Gerron about it."

He nodded and rose as she picked up a book. He bowed to her in good night, then, on impulse, kissed her cheek and sprinted for the door.

"Scamp!" she protested as he beat it out the doorway. "Don't be too noisy. I do like my beauty sleep," she called after him. "Not that it ever made a difference," she added in a mutter he almost missed.

Rowan slowed his pace a good dozen feet down the hall-way, exhaustion and exhilaration warring for control. He needed sleep and rest, but he had too much to do in his scant few human hours. Tomorrow, he would need to return to his brothers. It would be a long swim to Birney, but he *was* getting himself and his brother, and his little brother's sweetheart, cured. Rowan sighed wistfully as he walked toward the kitchen for dinner and the butler. He had to admit this princess was a beauty. His little brother knew how to pick them. And the king must like Max, since he let his daughter ride in his lap.

CHAPTER 6

"Are you sure you want to do this?" Max picked Tala up as the boat drifted far from Birney's shore. They'd gone beyond where they'd last seen sharks —and so beyond her kingdom. Was it possible Malosi had gotten the sharks to behave so unnaturally?

Tala tightened her grip on the injured guard's spear. "Yes. None of us have a choice." They'd talked with King Basil long into the night, but no other option had presented itself. He didn't want her to go, but what else could she do?

Max's jaw clamped and a flash of guilt darkened his eyes before he stepped closer to the bow. "Be careful, Tala." He dropped her over the side, and she splashed into her beloved sea and began swimming, a balance of speed and stamina.

Lily and King Basil had promised to take care of the injured guard and had sent a servant secretly to Litvania to warn Lysander and try to talk sense into Meilani. It was all they could do, and all Tala could do was not get eaten by sharks or orcas or get caught in fishing nets before she could tell her uncle and king about Malosi's treachery. She'd never swum so far alone before, and she'd never approached from this area. She didn't know its dangers and safe havens, and she very soon felt that lack of knowledge.

She'd barely gone a mile into the deep—it was still mostly empty water rather than reefs and creatures—when a change in the water signaled danger, above and behind. She twisted around, spear in front of her, and found three sharks racing toward her.

Tala spun and fled, swimming as fast down as she could. Merfolk and sharks could swim at about an equal rate, but she'd hardly swum at all for the past three weeks, and she could already feel the burn of her muscles.

Please! I've got to get through! Kingdoms depend on it!

She soon saw a reef on a shelf of rock, but it offered nowhere to hide, and her search of it slowed her down. A shark lunged for her, but she bolted away, slamming into the coral, breaking it and gashing her side. But she did drive her spear into the shark's cheek. As it writhed, she rolled a broken piece of coral in the blood leaking from her side and threw it beyond the shark. The shark dove for it, and she, one hand clasping her side, fled again.

Below that shelf though was only empty water. Mile after mile, only emptiness surrounded her and darkness looked up at her. Pulses of water against her scales told her the sharks hadn't forgotten her and were gaining. Why were they so tenacious? And there should be a reef here! Had she completely missed her calculations?

There! Down and to the right was a coral reef with a gap that might be large enough for her but not the sharks.

Purpose as well as fear gave her new energy, and she sped forward, her side burning and muscles beyond tired. A large shadow fell over the water in front of her, but she didn't have time to note if it was a ship or a whale.

Water pulsed faster against her, but the coral was only a half-dozen body lengths away. She could make—

The shark chasing her from above dove, and she jerked to

the side, raising her spear. It curved to avoid the stone point, and she started to chase it. Water pulsed faster, insistent and unexpected, then pain shot through her as rows of teeth crunched down on her hip. One of the other sharks had caught up too.

Her tough scales offered more protection than human skin, but a full-grown shark could still break bones and rip off scales given the opportunity.

Tala cried out, trying desperately to get her body—injured and shocked by pain—to bring the spear around to the shark's eyes. She managed one hit and one more scream before a shadow fell over her and she remembered no more.

❧

The world was blurry as Tala awoke, and some of that was the result of white hot pain. So much and all along her body. *Keep fighting! Keep swimming! You must get to Crestfall!* She tried to move, but the agony stole her breath, and she could get nowhere.

"Shh. Quiet now. You're safe. We'll take care of you." It was a man's voice, kind and concerned, and strangely familiar in accent. It eased her fear, and she fell asleep again. For a time.

Again and again, she roused or dreamed one. There was always pain. Often that voice talking to her. Once, she had a vague impression, or a dream, of a handsome man leaning over her, a kindness and worry in his face to match the voice. There was something about him that reminded her of Max, less teasing and a bit older and more kingly, and she was torn between sorrow she hadn't reached her kingdom and relief she was in a friendly human one.

Then there was another dream of a white-haired woman with an aura of magic about her. There was chaos and movement, then quiet.

"You say *this* is the cursed princess?" the woman said.

"I saw her with my brother," answered the man with the kind voice. "Please, can you heal her? Can you make Crystim help her?"

"Do not mention this to him," came the quick reply.

Fire erupted in her side, as if someone were poking her bones themselves. They did not feel right somehow, but things were so hazy. Even her breathing was difficult.

"Her body is broken, Rowan," the woman said with the heaviness of loss, and Tala wondered if her mind, through her dream, was telling her she was dying. *Not yet! Not until my uncle knows!* "It's a miracle she survived you bringing her here. I am not a healer."

A warm hand grasped hers. "But, Aunt, she—"

"Rowan—"

"No, you can turn her back! Back human—you can rebuild her bones in the transformation. Please, Aunt. He can't lose her too."

There was a long silence, and Tala wished the dream would start again. She didn't want to die in silence.

"There might be a way," the woman said at last, weary. "But," she continued, likely cutting off some reply from the anxious man, "it will cost. She must still heal, and interfering with nature . . . "

"Yes?"

Tala asked the same. Would she lose her gracefulness when she swam? It was a high price, but one she'd gladly pay to return to her kingdom and family.

"Her voice. She won't be able to talk, Rowan. You could say the injury to her body will be healed slowly in her vocal cords. Is that what you want?"

"Yes, if it will save her!"

A cool hand clasp her other, and it was a strange sensation to be held by one pleasantly warm hand and one pleasantly cool.

"Then leave me to my work."

She heard a movement, a kiss, and a door hastily opened and closed. Then the pain flared, not the throbbing agony she'd had but an active kind, mixed with magic.

"I'm sorry, my dear," the woman said, her tone weary and sad, "but there is no other way. Don't be too hard on him." She placed a cool hand on Tala's throat. Pain spiked, shredding the dream. The last thing Tala heard was a bittersweet whisper, "Take care of my boys, child, and let them take care of you."

CHAPTER 7

Tala's throat ached when she woke, and she wondered vaguely if she'd caught some human disease. If so, perhaps they would let her hole up for a day or two in the little house built in the grotto's waters for Crestfall's ambassadors. It would be nice to be surrounded by the sea for an entire da—

A gasp intensified the ache in Tala's throat—she wasn't in Birney. She'd been chased by sharks, and then . . . ? She must have escaped, but everything since feeling a shark lunge for her was largely a blank. She had a vague impression she'd dreamed, but she was too tired to worry about dreams.

The question was, where was she? And could she still get her message to her king? From the softness under her and the warm weight on top, she guessed she was in a human bed. She tried to sit up and nearly toppled at an odd, unbalanced feeling. Hands caught her shoulders and laid her gently down. She opened her eyes to see a white-haired enchantress watching her, a hint of concern in her eyes, despite the hard set of her mouth.

"I'm glad you're awake," the woman said. "Try scooting to

the edge of the bed for me. It's been over a day, and Rowan needs to leave."

Though confused, Tala responded to the command in the words and attempted scooting her tail to the bed's edge. She winced at a strange, uncomfortable knocking of bone on bone midway down her tail. She tried again, this time getting the odd feeling she had two tails and they were tangling up, like those clumsy human legs on little children.

Rowan.

Back human . . . transformation.

She froze at the remembered words, plucked from her dreams, and threw back the blanket covering her. An over-sized nightgown was hiding her body, and she hastily drew it up and gasped. Instead of her beautiful, graceful, sapphire blue tail, were two pale, spindly . . .

No!

"They're called legs, dear." The woman patted one of them, and Tala felt it.

No! Please no!

But she felt it. Those things were hers. *Were* her.

She was human.

Human. Human. The word rang through Tala's mind, relentless in its hammering. *Humans killed my parents. Humans have no scales. Humans can't breathe underwater. Humans can't live underwater.*

She was human. She could never tell her king of the danger to his life and kingdom. She could never go home.

Aunt Tiare! Uncle Fetu!

Tala opened her mouth, though to scream or to tell herself to wake up she wasn't sure. And it didn't matter, as nothing came out.

She clutched her aching throat. *What was happening? Why?*

Her breaths coming faster and faster, Tala forced herself to study the lady before her. From the flowing white hair to the shapeless black dress and curved sword, to the mansion surrounding her, there was only one person this could be: Lady Octavia, the *Moiwahine*, the feared Queen-Guard of the Sea. Likely the one person in existence able to turn a mermaid into a human or a human into a mermaid. Why would an enchantress more legendary than real, suddenly come into her little life?

"Why?" Tala mouthed as tears formed in her eyes, a very unmermaid-like reaction.

The woman just shook her head sadly. "It was the only way."

"My kingdom—" she mouthed, adding gestures she hoped were understandable.

"They'll look after it. But we must hurry now. Dawn is coming, and it is a long trip."

Tala grabbed Lady Octavia's wrist to get her attention, then made a motion with her hands, like she was snapping a piece of driftwood.

"All spells must have an end. What is mine?"

There was that sad smile again, and the woman tapped a pendant Tala hadn't noticed around her own neck. It was a single glittering blue scale wrapped in silver wire. "The end to your curse? The traditional end, if it were a curse, would be the kiss of a prince who loves you, and whom you love."

Tala drew back. Love a human prince? That would hardly free her to return to the sea!

Lady Octavia held up a simple dress the color of driftwood. "This is the best I could find. It belongs to one of my servants. I'll help you into it."

The words had a finality Tala couldn't shift, and she didn't respond with even a nod as Lady Octavia helped her change, then brushed her hair, braided it with surprising tenderness, and ushered in a young man.

As the stranger stood at the door, staring at her, some memory tickled her overwhelmed mind.

"You're not bleeding anymore. I'm glad," he blathered. "I hope you're feeling better. More yourself now?"

What a strange question. How could she feel more herself when she wasn't even *the same species*?

That sensation of familiarity tickled Tala again, and her dreams suddenly flooded back, jumbling up, but one part stood out above the rest: this man begging Lady Octavia to turn her human, even at the price of her voice.

This man, he had cost her—and maybe her kingdom —*everything*. How could someone with such a kind face and soothing voice be so cruel? There was something about Malosi that had always warned her about his true nature, but this man didn't have that. *Why?*

The young man's forehead wrinkled as if in confusion. "I'm going to take you back to Birney now," he said with a forced smile, and Tala jerked. Birney? "It's almost a day's travel. We have just enough time to get the boat and leave. I won't be able to speak with you for a while, but I'll get you to my brother . . . though I may regret it."

He winked, and she snapped her teeth at him in warning. *Stay away!*

For a moment she thought she'd won, but though taken aback, he still dared cross the room. She was opening and closing her mouth, her anger and confusion trying to force out words that couldn't come, when he scooped her up and hurried out to a pier on which floated a strange boat. Lady Octavia followed with a picnic basket, blanket, and parasol.

"I'll have you home in a jiffy." He carried her to the boat, speaking as if she were some frightened pet that needed comforting. She fisted her hands and flexed her feet—she could move a little better now. "I'm a fast swimmer. Lady Octavia was gracious enough to provide lunch for you." His forehead bunched again as she glowered at him. "And yes, the boat looks odd—I built it from spare timber—but it floats. Trust me."

Not on your life, Tail Thief!

She wiggled in his arms as he tried to sit her down in the bottom of the boat. Strength had been building in her since waking, and when he was forced to lower her to a standing position—him protesting the whole time about the stability of the boat—she planted her pale human feet on the flooring, stood for the first time ever, and shoved him over the side. He fell with a cry, landed with a splash, and disappeared into the waves. *May you grow fins and never see your home again!* She wobbled herself, the boat rocked, and she tumbled over the other side.

CHAPTER 8

Rowan couldn't figure out his brother's sweetheart. She'd appeared furious when she saw him, and yet so mournful now as she ran her fingers through the sea. But why? He'd saved her life! And gotten her uncursed, even if it would take time for her body to fully heal and her voice return. Of course, she'd been through a lot with the curse and shark attack—which had scared the daylights out of him even before he realized who she was and charged the sharks. Had she not been lucid after all when he'd introduced himself when they arrived at Lady Octavia's? Did she think *he'd* attacked her as a whale?

A spike of fear returned as he remembered seeing her in the shark's jaws, caught by one and about to be the object of a fight between three. She'd been so badly hurt. He'd gently scooped her up and swum faster than he thought possible to Lady Octavia's, dragging them both to shore the final half mile, her limp and bleeding.

His vision wasn't that great as a whale, especially not the long distance vision he'd been using when he'd seen his brother riding on the beach with a lovely brunette in his lap, but he *knew* this was the same woman. There was something unique about the luster of her hair and her figure, the way she held herself. Max had claimed the curse was something other *folk* also endured; Rowan had been shocked to see that the curse had been turning the lady into a merfolk. Given what he and his brother had been turned into, and Crystim's association with the rogue Crestfall noble, he shouldn't be surprised. Was that Crestfall traitor hoping to force a marriage alliance with Princess Lily?

What was she doing in the ocean anyway, come to think of it?

A horrible idea suddenly had anger fueling his large body through the waves. Surely this Princess Lily wasn't playing his brother and she *wanted* the alliance with that traitor? Had she been going to meet the merman?

Yet Max didn't lose his head over every pretty girl he met. Could she only be on shore so long?

Something odd-feeling about the skin of his head suggested that if human, his forehead would be creased with wrinkles, something his brothers told him he did a lot.

She pushed me off a boat. A woman with a little spunk was a good thing, but a cruel and capricious one was not.

Which was she? For his brother's sake, he very much hoped the former.

Do come for a visit and tell me how it goes, Lady Octavia had told him quietly before they left. *I expect wedding bells. Literal ones if you don't mind. I collect bells. I love the different sounds they make. Almost as lovely as a multitude of voices. And I can turn these on and off, which is a great advantage. Mage Isle doesn't get all in a tither about them either.*

Well, Lily was his brother's concern, not his. Rowan mentally shook his head and focused on swimming. She was back in her true form now, whatever her emotional state, and soon his brothers would figure out how to get that crystal ball.

Guessing it to be somewhere around midday, he slowed

his pace, letting the boat he'd been towing via a rope-encir-
cled board in his mouth drift serenely. It would be easier for
the girl to eat if the boat was fairly still. He made what he
hoped was a cheerful sound and disengaged from the boat.
He dove deep, cleared off predators from the area, and swam
a bit, eating krill as he did.

When he gently surfaced a little ways from the boat, the
woman had her back to him. He got the feeling that was
intentional, but at least she was eating, even if she looked at
each piece of food as a strange and dangerous thing. Had her
time as a mermaid addled her human memories? The slump
of her shoulders was so melancholy it made his own heart
ache.

He gave her as long as he dared for her meal before he
made another cheerful bellow—as quietly as he could, for
blue whales were loud creatures—and brought the boat back
into tow. Every so often, he glanced back to check on her.
She had the parasol up, and on occasion drank from the
canteen of water Lady Octavia had provided, but always, her
hand was in the sea.

As darkness came and Rowan felt the shrinking sensation
begin, he strained his eyes for the cove where he met his
brothers. The bay was deep and within walking distance of
the castle, but it was surrounded by tall cliffs and so not
useful for ships. There was, however, a waterfall at the end
and a small beach that made for a pretty little camping spot.
He scanned the coastline for the familiar silhouette, an odd
internal sense guiding his eyes.

There.

Rowan let the campfire on the shore guide him as he
moved behind the boat and nudged it closer to shore. He was
waddling himself up the sand, shrinking, shrinking, shrink-

ing, when he suddenly splashed into the water as himself. *I've got a surprise for you, Max.*

A gangly young man came crashing through the waves toward him, ready as his brothers always were to yank him from the water and into a hug. But this time, it was Max who was snagged into a fierce hug, caught by arms reaching desperately from the boat. Max, with a cry of surprised alarm, scooped the girl from the boat and started to lower her to the water, but she wrapped her arms tightly around his neck, effectively conveying a *no* to that. Max stiffened and carried her to the fire. As Rowan staggered to his feet, forgotten, a horrible foreboding this reunion wasn't going to go as he'd imagined settled in his gut. Why did Max seem more worried than joyous?

"Tala!" Max cried in alarm as he set her on a blanket. "What happened? You don't feel right. You . . . "

Who? The princess's name was Lily.

The girl pulled her dress up to her knees, pointing furiously at her legs, her throat, and at Rowan, the mix of despair and anger he'd seen in her earlier giving sharpness to her gestures.

"My brother did *what*?" Max roared as he spun on Rowan, now only a foot away.

Rowan didn't know what was going on, but he knew his brother well enough to duck the punch that would have bruised his jaw.

"What!" Rowan exclaimed as he backed away.

"You went to Lady Octavia, didn't you?" Max advanced on him, fist ready. "You went to the sea witch! And you helped her curse an innocent mermaid! Did you think this would help us some way? That Beau and I would accept such a deal?"

"She's not the witch Lady Porsche claims! And I didn't curse—I wouldn't—"

The image of the girl swimming so naturally even while fighting the sharks flashed before him. Had he . . . ?

Max's fist came flying toward his eye, and Rowan couldn't bring himself to move, a horrible guilt turning his body to lead. But then an eagle swooped down at them, screeching a protest, and Rowan landed on the ground in a pile with both his brothers. His big brother, Beau, pulled them to their feet, keeping them at arms' length.

"What are you two fighting about now?" Beau demanded. "We only have each other, remember? We don't have time for this. Our hours as men are too short." Beau, with a hand on each brother's collar, gave both a warning shake before releasing them.

Glaring bloody murder, Max jabbed a finger at Rowan. "He went to Lady Octavia and got a mermaid turned into a human who can't even speak! Tala, my *friend* and our only hope of warning Crestfall of a dangerous plot, which could lead to ruin for our kingdom eventually."

Was it really true? Rowan snapped around to the woman sitting on the blanket, watching them, one hand on her pale throat.

The hand he'd seen trailing through the water all day, the gesture so wistful. As if mourning the sea she was no longer a part of.

What have I done? He hadn't just changed her body and lost her her voice, he'd stolen everything.

He'd taken her home from her.

CHAPTER 9

Tala's heart was still racing as the men argued. Max had nearly put her in the water. The ocean—*her* ocean—had tried to kill her when she'd fallen off the pier earlier. Instead of feeling at home, her whole body easing at its touch, her eyes had stung and her lungs burned with the threat of death. Even more than seeing her legs, that had told her she really was human. Exiled.

Tala inched farther from the shore, and hated both her cowardice and the curse that caused it. *I want to go home. Will I see you again, Aunt Tiare? Uncle Fetu?*

The man who'd gotten her cursed stared at her as Max explained his crimes. *He* was one of her beloved Max's brothers?

In the firelight, she could see his whole posture wilt as his younger brother yelled at him and his older brother questioned him. For the first time in her life, Tala wanted to see someone beaten. There was a warning voice in her mind that claimed she was being unfair, that there was something important she was overlooking, but that hot ball of anger inside didn't want to listen. And how could one forgive something like this? This changed her entire life! And others'.

"I thought she was your princess and that I was curing her curse!" Rowan protested.

"Lily is hideously ugly!" Max roared, his concern for her a balm she desperately needed. She had no one but him, Lily, and King Basil in the whole human world.

"But I saw this woman riding in your *lap*. What was I supposed to think?"

"That she's a mermaid and can't ride a horse! I told you the mermaid ambassador was staying at the castle too and was often with us. She's a friend!"

"No, you didn't!"

"Yes—"

"He wasn't here then, Max," Beau said quietly. "Calm down, both of you. What's done is done. We can't wallow in guilt"—he looked pointedly at Rowan here—"or"—he turned to Max—"stew in anger. We can only see what's to be done now."

The younger brothers both took a calming breath and ran their fingers through their hair in an amusingly similar manner, or what would have been entertaining under other circumstances.

"The mage who cursed Princess Lily is cowering at Lady Octavia's," Rowan said. "He's also made a deal with a Crestfall merman, sirens, and Litvania. Lady Octavia said something about a crystal ball that could help us hidden in an egg. With it, we could free Princess Lily, ourselves, and threaten Litvania into good behavior."

Max and Beau shared a look. With a heavy sigh, Max said, "Rowan and I will go to the castle and explain to King Basil what's happened. Beau, look after Lady Tala." He resettled that brown cap of his on his head, and after Beau slipped him a leather journal, he jogged toward the cliff path. "Come on, Rowan, we need to hurry."

Rowan turned to her instead, and even in the firelight she

could see a hopeless look on his face, a useless apology forming on his lips.

Tala crossed her arms and turned away.

There was a long pause before Rowan said, wearily, "Fix her some warm tea please, Beau. Her throat probably aches. There should be some in the basket in the boat."

She flinched at that kindness but stared at the water until the two men were gone.

A few minutes later, Beau handed her a steaming cup of tea and a plate of fish and fruit and settled across from her with his own meal.

"Rowan isn't usually impulsive," he said, studying her. "He must have been very concerned about something. And Lady Octavia isn't cruel, despite the rumors. Why did they really turn you into a human, Lady Tala?"

Concerned? Why really? She was tempted to bristle and turn away at being questioned, but he was Max's brother, an heir to a throne. It was a fair question, too, one she'd been avoiding all day. She remembered sharks closing in and having trouble finding a reef in which to shelter. One shark got alarmingly close. After that things grew blurry. But it seemed like—

Tala pressed a hand to her chest, her breaths heaving, her heart thundering. This was nonsense. Was he trying to scare her?

What did it matter in the end? She was cursed and lost to her home, and it was Rowan's fault. She'd been chasing a shark away—for a chased shark rarely struck that merfolk again—when something grabbed her and she woke as a human. It was probably the whale that grabbed her. He probably wanted to earn King Basil's favor. Well, that had failed.

She noted Beau's gaze lowering from her face to where she clasped her throat. It wasn't the ache of a sickness she felt there. It was more like being run through by a narwhale.

Remember, it seemed to urge. She shook her head instead, willing the pain to retreat. *There is nothing else to remember.*

"Because he's an idiot who meddles in other people's affairs," she mouthed. She picked up her tea and turned her back on the prince.

Tala, that is not how a Grayrock behaves. She could almost hear her uncle calling her to courage and kindness. Well, she wasn't a Grayrock anymore. Grayrocks were merfolk, and she was human.

"Lady Tala," Beau said sternly, but Tala didn't turn around. "Grieve your loss, but do not by anger and bitterness, by pettiness, make the life you have now any worse than it must be. Or encourage my brother to bear guilt not his."

The words stung, but Tala just drank her tea and curled up on her side.

☙❧

They waited in silence for what seemed like hours before the sound of a group of men and horses drifted into the cove. Beau called a warning. Max returned a greeting. Soon, a party perhaps a dozen strong, accompanied by several horses laden with supplies, descended the cliffs into the cove.

As they neared the fire, Tala recognized Max, Lily, and King Basil himself. The latter greeted her as he drew his horse to a halt and began to dismount. The frail man's guards cast worried looks at him and kept near enough to catch him.

To her relief, King Basil did not require their assistance, and as soon as Tala saw her uncle's best friend was steady, she scrambled up—with Beau's help—flung herself into his arms, and sobbed into his chest. He patted her hair and thankfully did not tell her that being human wasn't so bad.

"There, there," he said when her tears subsided. "Should I

give the blackguard a black eye for you? Or should I hire my own mercenary mage to turn him into a frog so you can squish him with those unsightly things called feet? A whale is rather too large for that, after all."

A whale . . . Tala looked around for Rowan, but not seeing him, she glanced at the tinkered-together boat. The man who'd cast her from her home also knew what it was like to be exiled and transformed against his will.

Good.

King Basil handed her a handkerchief, and Tala wiped her face, somehow feeling much better, even though nothing had changed.

"Well?" King Basil pressed, his eyes searching hers.

Yes, a black eye! Another curse! I need a target for my pain.

Ashamed but unwilling to deny her spite, she gave no response. What did it mean that Rowan hadn't returned?

King Basil's lips turned down in a worried frown, and he faced the group. This time Tala noticed a woman she didn't recognize among them. Her gown was ridiculously large, though lovely with its violet hue and crystals sewn into it, making it sparkle in the firelight. It was almost as pretty as a tail. She was beautiful too, young and yet ageless, unless one studied her eyes. There was something very old about them as she looked at Tala. *Enchantress.* Tala knew it as instinctively as she knew this woman was not like the mage who cursed Lily.

The enchantress's gaze swept over the group, and Tala got the odd feeling she was cataloguing their attire. Was this Lily and Lysander's fairy godmother? Rumor had it she was clothing-obsessed and flighty, but kind. Could she help Lily, now that she was finally here?

"Lady Violetta," King Basil said, "may I present Prince Beau of Danskov and Lady Tala of Crestfall? Lady Violetta has been away on Mage Isle business, but she is now ready to help Lily with her curse and aid us in our other troubles."

"There is only so much I can do, I'm afraid." Lady Violetta gave Lily and Beau an apologetic look. "Rules and regulations being what they are, particularly regarding the godchildren of other enchantresses. However, I will do my best."

"What do you plan to do, Lady Violetta?" Beau asked.

"That," she said, her eyes glittering as her snow-white mare shook its mane, "is something I cannot tell. I've taken everyone's measurements, though, and will return in a few days. I believe I know just what will do the trick. Prince Rowan was vastly helpful. A mermaid on the loose in the human world is a dangerous thing to hearts, after all."

Meilani. Tala had to get to Litvania. She had to convince her, somehow, to give up her curse and go home. Meilani was spoilt and needed to learn how to care for others and to face the consequences of her selfish actions, before they cost more than she and others could pay.

And she needed to see Malosi pay for his treachery.

"Well," Lady Violetta said with a bright smile, "do watch for me and don't give up heart." She gave Tala a surprisingly serious look and disappeared in a flare of violet and silver.

"Taken our measurements? Is she judging our character?" Beau repeated in confusion as the glow faded. For a long moment, everyone stared at the empty spot where the enchantress had been.

King Basil cleared his throat. "She's better known for clothes than . . . Well, I sometimes wonder if her flighty reputation is purposeful, but . . . Well, while we look forward to Lady Violetta's aid, let's continue on here. We have several issues to deal with and ways to attack them.

"The shark infestation has prevented visits from Crestfall and kept our brave Lady Tala from telling King Aleki of Ambassador Malosi's treachery and Princess Meilani's foolish escapade. To combat that, Prince Rowan has volunteered to take, in his whale form, our injured merman guard home. They'll carry with them a written explanation of all that has happened. Our message *will* get through."

Tala gasped, and King Basil squeezed her hand.

He glanced at Lily, who stood on Tala's other side, one arm around her waist, keeping her steady. "Another challenge is my daughter's curse and gaining the egg with this powerful crystal ball." He pulled a leather journal from his jacket and handed it to Beau with a grateful nod. "Prince Maximillian shared with me tonight how his older brother has used his time as an eagle."

"In a way I hope Litvania will long have cause to regret." Beau's normally solemn expression turned downright sly before he smoothed it into a more kingly one and accepted the journal.

"Yes, my boy, they will," King Basil replied with a determined look before turning to Tala. "He's made a study of their fortifications and movements. The latter includes sending men across our border and stationing them near the Golden Tower and along the path to it. We suspect they are as much to blame for the injuries to our competitors as the bull. We believe they have also discovered the mage's crystal ball is in the egg and intend to steal it for themselves. Perhaps Ambassador Malosi intends to take the challenge himself in time."

Tala huffed. Of course Malosi would trick a mercenary mage into making a power source like that accessible. Was he hoping to conquer both land and sea for himself, using it to make himself human or merman as he wished?

"To deal with this, I would like to announce that there will be one more attempt to save my daughter from her curse. Prince Maximillian of Danskov has volunteered, and I have accepted. I will send my own men to clear the way to the Tower, and send Max a guide and trainer, the best I know."

Tala tugged on King Basil's sleeve. "What of me? What of Meilani and Malosi and Litvania?" she mouthed and tried to mime. His brows furrowed as he studied her, and Lily whispered something in his ear. A paternal frown tugged his lips down even as he gently patted her hand.

"And that brings us to our beloved ally Crestfall and my grandson in Litvania." King Basil's jaw tightened, and Tala got an image of him as a younger man, as a fierce warrior. "Instinct warns that messages will not reach my grandson unhindered. It is best we sneak in. They are hosting balls all month. It is my wish a prince of Danskov will escort Lady Tala to a ball so she can talk sense into the princess and get her away from Malosi's influence. Hopefully by then, Crestfall will advise us what to do about him. Prince Beau will spend his days gathering information and passing along messages to let us keep track of one another."

Her godfather gave her a proud look, and purpose stiffened her spine. Tail or no tail, she was not useless.

"We brought horses. You may begin your journey tomorrow, first to the Golden Tower, as it is on the way, then Litvania. My guide will catch up to you. As soon as we've caught up with him," he added in a mutter.

Tala's spine lost its strength, and the whole, big human world bore down on it. Lily pulled Tala into a hug, and Tala stumbled into her, her spindly legs as weak as her resolve.

Ride a horse? Alone? Go to a strange city? To a ball? Leave the shore for the mountains?

Stop moping, Tala. Do what you must. The crystal ball could save you too.

Could it?

Tala touched her aching throat. Some memory or dream warned that returning to a mermaid now would be her doom. But Tala ignored it. She lowered her hand to the scale pendant and once again stiffened her spine. She'd survived her parents' deaths. She'd survived three weeks as a pet mermaid in a human kingdom. By typhoon or tides, she would survive this. She would help save kingdoms *and* find a cure for herself that did not involve a prince, and when her voice returned, she would find Prince Rowan and chew him out until he felt like a tree sent through the paper mill.

CHAPTER 10

Tala woke inside a tent with Lily's hideous face entirely too close. Her friend held out a cup of tea, which smelled strangely appealing, but human tea had never tasted good.

"Good morning, Tala! I brought you my favorite breakfast tea."

Tala wrinkled her nose, and Lily rolled her eyes.

"What did you expect when you insisted we used boiled sea water? This is made with fresh water, and I assure you, it is much better."

"Of course I wanted it in sea water—I drank, swam in, and *lived* in sea water," Tala mouthed sharply as she sat up. She could say whatever she wanted to now, and she fully intended to make use of that. Her whole body ached from riding the horse—and falling off it until Max made her ride with him. And she missed her morning routine at home with her aunt.

A slight quirk of Lily's lips made her narrow her eyes at her.

"What?" she mouthed as she ran her fingers through her hair. Human hair was not so lustrous as mermaid hair. It was dull and tangled easily. Her skin was softer though, like a baby merfolk's before their scales formed. Not that it mattered. She would *never* like being human.

Lily smiled innocently. "I'd be furious too, you know."

Tala gave her another sharp look and ran her fingers faster through her hair. "You're not going to use reverse thinking to talk me into believing being a human is better than being a mermaid! That I should *stay* human." Tala glanced past Lily to the tent opening, through which she could see Max and Beau, but thankfully not Rowan. She'd heard the others hoping he'd join them today, and heard their whispers that 'poor Rowan' was smitten with her. "And you're certainly not going to convince me of any romantic nonsense about Prince Rowan. 'I know just the one,' Max said. Well, Rowan may look handsome and kind, clever and just a bit of a tease, but I am not so foolish. I know better. He-he—he's nothing but a dumb whale!" Despite how safe his voice in her dreams had made her feel, which made the truth of him even more horrible.

Lily's smile grew. "You think he's handsome?"

Tala's fingers stilled in her hair, and her wide eyes met her friend's.

"I would never try to convince you to stay human," Lily said, a sly look in her eyes. "I don't *need* to—not when the view from our mountaintops, moonlit walks in the forest, dances with handsome and kind princes, and chocolate cakes and peach pies can do it for me."

Tala narrowed her eyes and pointed from her lips to Lily's ears.

Lily shook her head, yet touched her own ears and gave her a wry smile. "I've a confession to make. I don't hear well. Haven't since a childhood illness. I rely a lot on lip reading. So, for me, you still talk!"

Tala blinked at her friend for a long moment, then groaned. The one thing she was looking forward to—saying whatever she wanted, not having to hold her tongue—and even that was foiled!

When Lily, probably a mind-reader too, chuckled, Tala sighed. No. This was a good thing. "I'm sorry about your hearing." She patted Lily's hand, but her friend shrugged.

"Me too." Lily tugged thoughtfully at her ear a moment before continuing, "I whined after it happened, and then I adjusted." She gave Tala an intent look, which Tala, like a lot of things recently, chose to ignore.

Lily set the teacup down and rose, a mischievous smile back in place. "One day, Tala, you're going to have to eat crow when you admit Rowan really saved your life." Tala cocked an eyebrow, and Lily's mirth faded into seriousness. "He's really nice you know. He's a blend of Max's humor and Beau's kingly sternness, and an ingenuity all his own. He'd be perfect for you, and I'm not just scheming to keep you near. We won't force it, of course, but we wanted to point out the possibility."

Tala mouthed, "Not on my life," very clearly, then made a shooing motion, and Lily patted her shoulder and left her alone to change. Human clothes were an oddity. Merfolk usually only wore jewelry, though occasionally they would wear seal skin if the waters turned cold, but humans had layer upon layer.

After finally wrestling her awkward body into equally awkward clothes, Tala emerged from the tent and found Max leading her horse to her. Her backside ached, and she stifled a moan. Why did humans choose mounts that made them sore in places mermaids didn't even have?

"Surely the great sea horse rider can handle a land horse," Max mocked with a smile. He held the creature still before her.

Tala shot him a look, accepted the quiet Beau's hand up, and settled onto the horse. She could do this. She would. For the honor of mermaids.

The horse nickered, and Tala leaned forward to gently rub the mare's neck. The beast's fur was so soft, unlike the tough scales of a sea horse. The latter glided smoothly through the water though, no bouncing at all, which was decidedly in its favor.

The mare gave her mane a good shake and stamped a foreleg, and Tala could almost feel her energy and readiness to run. She could charge mountains, this one. A hint of a smile touched Tala's lips. She remembered that feeling, though for her childhood self it was exploring some channel of the sea floor or a shipwreck with her parents or aunt and uncle. And once or twice, if she dared admit it, she'd dreamed of climbing mountains and castle stairs too.

"Ready?" Max, with a glance at her hand in the mare's mane, winked at her, and Tala smothered the smile and sat upright. The scamp laughed as he mounted his horse. He made a waving motion, and they set out on a narrow trail through the woods, a little-used path that led, after many days' travel, to the Golden Tower and from thence to Litvania.

❦

Tala was bone weary by the end of the day. She hobbled from the horse to a boulder between the cliff and the shore of the sheltered cove in which they were to camp and sat. Lily soon joined her, her walk more graceful than Tala's limping gait. Together, they watched the men set up camp. Half the guards had stayed atop the cliff on duty, but two aided Max with the tents as one worked on a fire to warm the chill night air blowing in off the sea.

As the salt-tinged breeze washed over her, soothing her warm skin, Tala had to admit—and she hated to do so—that the forest had been all Lily claimed. The tangy scent of fir and pine, the earthy smell of disturbed dirt, the crispness of a mint leaf Max had found, it had all been there. And then there were the sights and sounds: sunlight filtering through the tree canopy, myriad hues and shapes belonging to an enormous variety of plants, the splashing of a brook, the colors and songs of birds, the view at a crest in the trail . . .

Tala pressed a hand to her heart, in which had started an ache for home akin to a boulder pressing her into the sand. Trying to find the good in this was foolish—it was making all she'd had as a mermaid less, her loss less, and she wouldn't accept that lie.

Is it really diminishing it though? Couldn't both worlds have good? Was her loss any less if there were still beautiful things in her life?

Tala rammed that chest of thoughts shut and instead moaned about her sore muscles. Horses. Bah!

Bah? Really, Tala, is that who you want to be?

She slammed the lid again, an act made easier as Max strolled over and promptly handed her and Lily each a curry comb. He'd decided everyone needed a job, and since Tala theoretically agreed work was good, she hadn't been able to complain when he'd set them to grooming the horses in the shade of a copse of trees at the cliff base. *Learning to see beyond ourselves to others, even to our mounts, is important*, he'd said as he explained how to care for the horses and check their hooves.

"I know Beau will be spying for us and reporting to my grandfather at night," Lily mused as the three worked, "but I wonder if Rowan will be able to find the cove and join us. Papa told him of every one we'd stay at until we had to move inland."

Tala scowled and brushed a little faster along her mare's side. Couldn't the human stay away? Did she have to see him every night as well as deal with his curse on her?

"I hope so." Max lifted his horse's hooves one by one to check them for stones and injuries. "Beau at least has purpose as an eagle, and can see and hear people talking. Rowan can only swim. No one should be alone so much and without purpose."

Only swim? There was the beauty of the sea to enjoy!

But even as she said it, Tala remembered the empty stretches, the dangers, the cold streams, the tight places keeping a whale from getting too close to her city and all the warmth and comfort it offered. His days would be long and lonely, wouldn't they?

"I wouldn't want to be alone all day every day," Lily said, and Tala's heart twisted despite herself. Was she being too harsh? "Maybe the fire will help him find us, even if he has to change in the sea and sail the boat in."

"He doesn't have the boat." Max lowered the hoof and fingered that floppy brown hat of his, his brows furrowed in concern as he looked out over the crashing waves. "He couldn't take it and get the merman home. We can only hope he'll reach us in time."

Following his gaze, Tala winced. Rowan had left his safety measure for the sake of her people?

She opened her mouth to ask how long he'd been cursed to be a whale, when her throat hurt, reminding her of her loss. Her fingers seeking out the scale pendant, she set her jaw and went back to grooming the mare. If Rowan hadn't been so foolish in his "help" of her, he wouldn't be in this predicament. She had no reason to feel for him. All that mattered was keeping her kingdom and Birney safe and getting home to her aunt and uncle. She suspected her uncle set her up as ambassador to keep Malosi from asking King Aleki for her hand in marriage. There was no need to worry about that now—the traitor would die. She'd go home to Crestfall and never leave again. She'd lost her home and family once; she wouldn't lose them again.

As she worked, she sensed Max and Lily look at one another over the horses, some message passing between them, something that included her, but Tala focused on the mare's leg. The humans could think what they wanted. They didn't understand and would never try to. It was easier to tell her to get over it and be happy where she was. Having her aunt and uncle hadn't made the loss of her parents any easier, and she wouldn't let anyone tell her to pretend the good things of the human world made up for her loss.

Her lips flattened into a hard, rebellious line, effectively silencing all conversation as they finished their tasks.

Max was checking over her attempt at grooming when a splash was followed by a guard's cry.

The human had found them.

CHAPTER 11

The merman's wounds were bound and no longer bleeding, so why were the sharks so interested in him and Rowan? The creatures seemed more ubiquitous and aggressive now than even a few days ago.

Rowan charged one shark as the merman tied to his long body brandished a spear at another.

"This isn't natural." The merman spoke into the water, and it was strange hearing a voice where he was used only to the many non-word sounds found in the sea. "Some great evil has been done to them. Even our feared enemies must be respected and not controlled like this."

Was there something Rowan could do about it? Beau may have the air and Max the land, but to Rowan had been given the sea.

He tried vocalizing what he hoped would be understood as a question.

"The work of the mage through a magical treasure," the merman replied. "I will ask my king if we can send out a team of our bravest warriors to search for it."

That wouldn't be wise considering they were the hunted

and couldn't get far even when they weren't needing to defend themselves.

But Rowan had swum far and wide and deep in this ocean, and a memory was tickling his mind, trying to pull itself to the forefront.

The merman directed him down at a sharp angle, through a swimming ring of sharks, and to a canyon of the sea floor. Jutting rock and alert guards made entry to predators difficult, but Rowan could see through the barriers enough to discern an underwater kingdom that left him in awe. Merfolk of all colors swam gracefully within a city—a true city at the bottom of the sea. They'd wrought buildings and even arches of coral and shell, of driftwood and stone, atop and around and within natural formations of rock rising up from the ocean floor. It didn't have a hodgepodge look, but one of order and beauty. To aid the latter, the most beautiful of the stationary sea creatures hung like flowers on its walls and along its canals.

Rowan gave a pleased bellow.

"There is none like Crestfall even among our brother kingdoms," the merman replied proudly as two guards bearing tridents approached. He shouted a greeting Rowan did not understand, and soon the guards had sliced through the ropes holding him to Rowan.

They took him into the city, where Rowan could not follow. He swam the canyon, seeing what he could see of the far reaches of the city, eating krill, and chasing off sharks. Warm water rising up from the canyon cooled against his sides, hinting at the paradise hidden within the cold open ocean.

After a time, the blast of a horn—or shell, in this case— had him returning to what he likened to a gate.

Among a group of guards were an older couple, their scales turquoise edged with silver. Something about the woman's face reminded him of Tala, and he noted the compass necklace the man wore, a gift King Basil had said would identify Tala's uncle.

I stole your niece from her home.

You saved her life, Rowan.

Rowan struggled with the conflicting thoughts, with feeling and truth, as the couple slowly approached. He half expected the man to raise a spear at him, but he only held out a small, ornate wooden chest.

The couple halted a dozen feet from him, studying his eye as if they could see the real him through it.

The woman suddenly swam to him, touched a hand gently to the skin beside his eye, then turned and fled. If she'd been human, she'd be crying, and he hated seeing ladies cry. *You are a blackguard, Rowan, a blackguard. You can even make mermaids you don't know weep.*

The man looked after her a long moment, then held up the box. When Rowan nodded his long head, he tied it in the remaining ropes. He didn't immediately leave though, but studied Rowan, as if intrigued by a whale close up. He leaned nearer to him.

"Well done, my boy," he whispered. "Tell Tala we'll visit as soon as we can. And if you find any more transformation spells, I would love to walk the human world. Tala and my wife do as well; they're simply too stubborn and sentimental to admit it. But if anyone can help my niece see it, it'd be you, Rowan of Danskov, inventor-prince."

If Rowan had been human, he would have gaped. As it was, he swallowed an unusual amount of sea water.

"You saved her life and changed her days," the merman continued, "you can change her heart as well. In the best ways, if what I have heard of you is true." He patted a shocked Rowan on the side. "King Basil, as a good grandfather should, spied on all the eligible princes of the neighboring kingdoms and liked your family in particular. He has also long promised me a horse, a dog, and a cat if I could manage to gain legs, and I've always wanted a horse, a dog, and a cat."

Before Rowan could vocalize anything, though he didn't know what to say, the merman winked at him, bowed, and followed after his wife, leaving Rowan alone with a treasured chest.

⚜

Rowan was dog tired by the time he dragged himself ashore at Lady Octavia's. In fact, he was human tired, whale tired, *and* dog tired.

He shook himself of sea water like a dog and trudged up the sandy shore to where his step-aunt and Crystim waited. He shed the ropes still attached to him as he went, only keeping hold of the one to which Tala's chest was secured.

"And how is our pelagic prince?" The mage's condescending look vanished as Rowan hauled Tala's chest in and picked it up. Alarm flickered through the man's eyes. Interesting.

Lady Octavia's hand glowed with a flame, making the jewels encrusting the chest sparkle, and Crystim's concern eased. Very interesting, especially since Rowan had once seen a plain chest of similar size at an unlikely spot along the offshore border between Litvania and Birney.

"The pelagic prince is getting along swimmingly, thank you, Crystim," Rowan said with a smile. "Good evening, Aunt." Rowan met her eye, trying to keep his suspicions about the shark infestation and his roiling emotions regarding a certain mermaid in check. *I have much to discuss with you.* She returned a subtle nod.

"What is that you have?" Crystim took a step forward, such an eager look in his eye Rowan was surprised he wasn't rubbing his boney hands together in anticipation of collecting the box for himself.

63

Rowan shifted the chest to his other side, away from Crystim. "I ran across a merfolk injured by sharks. Those have been oddly active of late. Have you noticed?"

"Merfolk or sharks?" Smug satisfaction undergirded his tone, and Rowan wondered if poison was adequate to kill a mage.

"Sharks," he said, an edge to his tone. "When I took him home, a couple from the city gave me this. It seems a daughter of Crestfall is now human, and they wish me to give this to her."

Alarm again flashed across the mage's narrow face, but it slipped swiftly into his typical condescension. "What an interesting day you've had, Prince Rowan."

"Yes, but one best discussed after the boy has had his dinner." Lady Octavia, who'd been studying them both, took the box and led them into the house. Rowan was once again dried at the doorway, but this time he was also sent off to find the butler for a spare set of clothes.

"Tell me more about the chest? Its design is simply stunning." Crystim's silence had lasted, surprisingly, until the main course, a fact Rowan was grateful for. How long had it been since he'd regularly enjoyed more than campfire meals with his brothers?

"That is all I can say about it. But why don't you tell me more about your portfolio? This bull that turns into a bird that must lay an egg that must be collected and presented to you. Does this bird perchance return to you after it is birthed from the bull?"

"Naturally, where else would it go?"

Rowan flashed his teeth at him. "As I was swimming around, enjoying the vast ocean stretches without another soul, it occurred to me how long and difficult of a quest it would be for a human to chase a bird across an ocean to an island you can only get to if touched by magic. How many princes and nobles fit that description? It's hardly sporting, now is it, ol' boy? One might think you'd rigged the quest to fail."

"Are you considering joining, Prince Rowan?" The mage scraped his spoon harshly over the bottom of his dish of custard.

"Not at all. It's the ethics of the matter that concern me." *And my aunt's flatware.*

The mage's responding laughter was as wince-inducing as his next scrape of spoon on dish. "Humans have such quaint ideas of ethics. When you live longer, you understand things better."

"I should think," Lady Octavia cut off Rowan's reply, "that would give you a better appreciation for ethics, given that those you've wronged have a greater chance of getting *their own back* over time."

A chill went down even Rowan's spine at that. *What has the worm taken from you, Aunt? Or tried to?*

CHAPTER 12

"T hat is an excellent point," Crystim said hastily.

"How would you, in your professional opinion," Rowan asked while the man was off-balance, "turn a mermaid into a human? That must take great skill." Rowan's stomach clenched in the silence that followed. During his long swims, he'd remembered a story of a mermaid who wanted to be human, a tale that Lily had told Max. It did not have a happy ending.

Crystim's Adam's apple bobbed, and he peeked at Lady Octavia before studying his custard. "Believe it or not, there's a very old spell for that. Quite ancient. It was a challenge for me to translate it. The language is not read anymore and the copy had started to fade and—"

"Does this mermaid turn to sea foam if she fails to gain the human's affection?" Rowan asked, his jaw tightening. *Max had mentioned Tala, her superior virtues and her exquisite artwork, when telling the story, and I'd not realized who he was talking about. If only I'd paid more attention!*

"Ah, I believe that is how the story goes, but this young mermaid is so beautiful and ambitious, it will be no problem for her to steal the prince's heart away from—I mean, win the prince's love."

Rowan's hand clenched under the table. It was all he could do to not look at his aunt. *Please don't have used that spell on Tala!*

Crystim set his spoon aside with a deliberateness that gained their attention. "I hate to put a damper on our lively spirits, but the time has come for me to leave." He smiled condescendingly at Lady Octavia, who regarded him cooly. "You have been a most gracious hostess, Lady Octavia. However, your nephew has stricken my soul with a conscience, and I must go to Litvania to be sporting about this egg business. I doubt it will make a difference in the end, but he is right that I should be there."

"I think that's very wise of you." Lady Octavia gestured to her austere, weather-beaten butler by the door. "Gerron will help you pack."

"That won't be necessary."

"Oh, but I insist. The island is difficult to find, and you don't want to forget anything. Gerron is also my master gunner and the sort of man to keep things in their proper place. He'll make sure nothing is misplaced."

Rowan bit back a scoff as Crystim paled. *After something here too, were you?*

Crystim laughed nervously as he laid his napkin aside. With a few more parting words, he bowed to Lady Octavia and left the room, the faithful Gerron at his heels.

Lady Octavia returned to her dessert, for which Rowan had lost his appetite. Had his insistence Lady Octavia "cure" Tala put her at risk of sea foam? *Trust your aunt's heart, Rowan. Think.* It was hard to think with the image of sea foam drying on the sand bludgeoning his mind. *Calm and think. Trust.*

It took more effort than he cared to admit, but Rowan

had managed to loosen his clenched fists by the time Lady Octavia laid aside her spoon.

"How is your human, Rowan?"

"You mean how is my *mermaid*?" he growled despite himself, then corrected himself. "How is *the* mermaid? She'd like to gut me and feed me to the sharks. You knew, didn't you?"

She didn't shy from his accusing gaze, only returned a heartbreakingly sad one that didn't ease his concern at all. "Of course I knew. It was the only way to save her . . . I'm sorry."

Sorry! As if that fixed things! "What are the terms, Aunt?"

"She will not turn to sea foam, Rowan." Lady Octavia's hand twitched, almost as if she thought to reach for his but decided against it. "Though I cannot guarantee that of the mermaid princess. A book of spells I'd written and lost many years ago was found in Crystim's luggage. He—"

"You wrote a spell to turn silly mermaids into sea foam for being curious?" Rowan exclaimed, his voice rising in pitch and volume.

"It is more than that, and less. It was written during a dark time of my life and was never meant to be used again. It will not happen to your mer—"

"Her name is Tala, Lady Tala of Crestfall."

"It will not happen to Lady Tala of Crestfall," she said in a calming tone Rowan tried to grasp and heed. "That was a genuine transformation."

A genuine transformation . . . I didn't sign her death warrant. She'll at least live. "There must be an end to it?"

"Of sorts." His aunt gave him an intent look. "She must choose to return the love of a prince. It's then she'll be free of what truly ails her."

"That would hardly help her return home."

"I suppose that depends on the prince. There aren't only human princes, you know."

A prick, unreasonably like jealousy, assaulted his heart. "That's all there are on land, to which she's now confined."

Lady Octavia made no reply to that bitter comment. Rowan sighed, and leaning on the table, ran his fingers through his damp curls. "She doesn't want to be human," he said at last, apology in his tone.

"We often face a thing we don't want, and yet in the end, discover it was best, or at least necessary."

Rowan huffed. "And there is much wisdom that will not soothe our hearts or days."

"The deer that feeds a hungry family through the winter must be fought for, Rowan. It is the same with truth—to change our hearts and soothe our days, we must fight for it. Capture it and study it day after day until it stays, believed."

Rowan's fingers stilled in his hair. *You know that. How hard did you work to believe you were forgiven after you broke Beau's leg, an injury that even now sometimes bothers him? Do it again with this, help her do it as well, if she will let you.* "I have a stubborn soul, Aunt. I'm sorry."

She leaned back in her chair with a huff. "So do we all. Do not worry about the end of her spell now, Rowan. She must heal. If she changes back too soon, it will not be good for her. Focus on saving the kingdoms and help her find her purpose again."

Her purpose? Rowan dragged his fingers through his hair once more, then sat up, placing his hands on the table. "Yes. That might help. To be adrift and far from home, without purpose, that is a terrible thing."

Perhaps he *could* help her, or at least empathize, if she'd let him. He felt a hand on his, surprisingly warm and comforting, dragging him back from his own dark first days as a whale. He looked up in surprise and saw Lady Octavia swiftly draw her hands back to her lap and rise from the table.

She strode to the wall bearing a museum of weapons he'd

longed to study and stopped before a spear, a king's or mage's weapon he was sure. As with most men, weapons drew him, and he joined her in admiring it. This weapon of kings was taller than she was, with blue-and-silver patterns of sweeping waves with various creatures crashing through them hammered into its shaft. On its bronze spearhead was the imprint of a city like that seen only beneath the waves.

She studied it a long moment, then, to his shock, plucked it from the wall and turned to him. "You might need this."

"But I—" *I'm only an ordinary human!* He reflexively accepted it anyway, and jumped at a zap as it touched his hand. Rather than make him loosen his grip, the zap caused his hand to firm about the shaft. It felt strangely right in his grip.

"Consider it a fishhook spell," his aunt said in a sly tone that dragged his eyes away from the spear. "That once belonged to a great merfolk king, and only one who has aided them can bear it."

Aided? A fishhook spell? He was lifting his hand from the spear to make sure it was possible when she caught his arm and urged him toward the door. "Come, let's go to the dock. And bring that. Let's watch Crystim squirm knowing what you have and what he does not—my lost spell book and the one he came to steal."

CHAPTER 13

Without even checking to see what or who was responsible for the splash, Max shot off toward the shore and was soon hauling a soaking wet Rowan, leaning heavily on a spear of all things, toward the fire. Rowan laughed as Max slapped him on the back, playfully scolding him for never making it all the way to shore and causing him to get wet to bring him in.

"Thanks to King Basil, I have clothes that actually fit you for tonight," Max said as Rowan stopped on the sand to shake himself of excess water like a bird bathing itself before continuing to the fire. Tala's eyebrows rose nearly to her hairline as the firelight illuminated Rowan's form. The human wore only trousers and shirtsleeves that clung to broad shoulders and a muscled torso, the better to swim in, though less than what a human typically wore.

She'd always suspected humans wore clothes because they found their unscaled bodies unattractive and flabby and too sensitive. But the play of wet fabric over muscle as Rowan thrust the spear into the sand and knelt before the flames suggested something else entirely. Mermen's scales ended above their hips, and they rarely covered their chests, but somehow, she imagined seeing a human man's chest would be different, far more intimate since it was normally concealed.

Rowan picked up a jacket from the pile of clothes by the fire, held it to his shoulders to gauge the size, then tossed it to the ground and began unbuttoning his wet shirt.

Tala felt a blush leaping to her cheeks, confirming her suspicion. Lily laughed, then called out, "Max! Warn your brother this isn't a bachelor camping party tonight."

With a startled cry, Rowan clutched his open collar, his wide eyes searching for them in the shadows beyond the fire. Tala inched back, deeper into them.

Max obligingly slapped his brother on the shoulder. "There are ladies and guards with us tonight, brother dear. Be on your best behavior."

"You could have warned me *before*!" Rowan sputtered as he re-buttoned his collar and slipped the dry coat on over his wet shirt. Lily stepped from the tree's shadows, waved, then dragged Tala, glower in place, out behind her. Rowan met Tala's eye and stiffened. If she wasn't imagining it, guilt and hurt both flashed across his face.

His impulsive foolishness got me cursed.

He wanted to apologize, and you wouldn't let him.

I have no voice because of him. My throat always aches because of him.

He spent all day alone and will soon spend his nights alone.

I am exiled too!

He broke her gaze to turn to Max, who, she'd not realized, was holding a box of some—hers. He was holding *her* art chest, a little human-made, jewel-encrusted chest she kept her carving and art tools in, that she'd left at home.

Rowan had gotten to her city then. Or near enough for Crestfall's gatekeepers to see the injured guard and help him inside. But the chest—he'd seen her aunt and uncle. How had the news of her curse hurt them? Were they despairing? She was all they had. Tala pressed a hand to her heart, her breaths gaining speed.

Rowan took the box from Max and stepped slowly around the fire toward her, his expression shuttered, his movements wary, as if he expected her to fly at him in a rage.

Did she deserve that reproach?

She pulled her hand from Lily's and planted her feet, the ache in her throat growing with each of his soft steps, the art chest held out before him like a trident aiming at her heart.

It couldn't have been easy for a whale to carry that box, much less a man swim with it. Why had he done it?

Why would her uncle and aunt give her treasure to him after what he'd done to her?

Rowan stopped a half dozen feet away and lifted the chest, making its gold trim glimmer in the firelight. "Your aunt and uncle send their greetings and a promise to visit as soon as you've returned to King Basil's palace."

She made no move for the box or any acknowledgement. What was there to say? Her aunt and uncle couldn't come anyway, not with the sharks.

"Lady Tala?"

Something in his voice snapped her gaze to his despite herself. His eyes were a dark brown, unlike the turquoise, greens, blues, and lavenders of merfolk scales and eyes. *Not like my people. Not to be trusted.* Tala raised her chin, her hand still clutched to her chest.

He flinched but held her gaze. "Forgive me. I didn't know or I . . . If there is anything I can do . . . " He choked on the words, enough guilt and sorrow in his eyes to bury a ship.

Her clenched fist loosened. Was he truly sorry, or merely worried about the consequences? And if she did forgive him . . .

If she forgave him, she'd be expected to get to know him, to treat him like any other human. Well, she wasn't going to.

He could stew in his guilt. She didn't want to be part of the human world.

Tala spun away and all but ran to her tent. Even if she didn't hate him, or knew she shouldn't, her heart ached too much to even look at him. Or at a chest from a home she might never be able to return to.

❧

Tala hadn't been curled up on her bed for two seconds when she realized she'd forgotten to close the tent flap. Her traitorous eyes refused to shut out the night, but rather turned back to where her conscience said she should still be.

Rowan walked slowly back to the fire, but instead of taking up the pile of dry clothes to change, he stumbled and sat, exhaustion in every line of his body. The box in his lap, he tapped his fisted hand against the sand, then snatched up a towel from the pile of garments and began fiercely rubbing his wet hair.

Max rested his hand on his brother's shoulder. Lily sat beside them, angled to see both. "I'm sorry, Rowan. I thought she would handle it better."

Tala's fist clenched the corner of her pillow. Who was he to judge? What did he know?

More than you want to believe, Tala. The quiet voice she'd been trying ignore finally broke through the walls in her mind, and Tala squeezed her eyes shut. *Your pain is not all that matters, child,* her aunt had more than once told her after she'd lost her parents. *Don't let it steal your ability to see others, to see purpose and beauty in life.*

"It's a lot to deal with, Max. The sea has its beauties. I can understand why she loves it now."

Shock opened Tala's eyes at the soft reply. Rowan was defending her? He understood?

"I don't disagree," Max said. "And we both know what

being forced to leave our home is like, but you and Beau don't—"

"I'm a whale, Max. I could cry buckets of tears every day and no one would know."

"Yes," Max agreed irritably, that loyalty she usually admired about him stinging tonight. "But you're not being rude and unreasonable."

"Give her time, Max. And yes, you know exile, but when your body is changed . . . when even a part of it is lost, it . . . " Rowan glanced at the sea, then scrubbed a hand over his face, his shoulders rounding.

"It's a different kind of loss," Lily said softly, the tip of her finger tracing the contour of her ear. "It can take time to heal."

"I know," Max said curtly. Leaning over the fire, he stirred a pot of soup an unobtrusive guard had started before leaving to pitch his tent. With a growl, Max tossed the spoon back into the soup pot. "It's just that you're my brother and you should be treated better. I expected better of Tala."

Tala sucked in a breath, Max's words sinking deep and stinging.

"There's no need to be upset," Rowan said tiredly as he continued to rub his temple.

"Why shouldn't I?" Max retorted, a rare sharpness to his tone. "Look at you. You're blaming yourself where I'd be flaming mad. We won't let you hide away in guilt this time, not like when you broke Beau's leg. You've asked for forgiveness where it counts. You walk with your head high now. No shame, no cowering. No running from her, from us."

Rowan scoffed, but he finally raised his head. "Who's running?" He picked up the dry clothes and stood. "Not that it matters. After tomorrow night, I'll stay with Lady Octavia. I thought I could help, but she needs time and space. I'll give her that. For now. I'll tell you what I can— she might listen to you." He started toward the trees, clothing in hand, but Max, voice rising in alarm, caught his arm.

"Rowan—"

Rowan stilled and wrapped his hand around the one on his arm. "No, Max." He met Max's eye, then gently pried his little brother's hand from his arm. "I promised King Basil I'd follow for at least two nights. I'll fulfill that, then I'll be gone. You'll be fine without Beau and me, she won't be as distressed, and I—I'm tired of long swims."

He spun away again, but this time it was Lily who arrested his flight.

"What happened, Rowan?" she asked, a deep concern in her tone that pulsed a warning of danger to Tala's carefully built wall. "Where was she when you found her?"

Tala grabbed her scale pendant, as if claiming it as witness. *Chasing away a shark. On my way home.*

As she ran her fingers over it, a crack on the back arrested her attention, and for the first time, she studied the pendant. It wasn't a single, perfect scale. It was two—one whole backed by one broken as only a strong predator determined to kill could.

Chasing away a shark. On my way home.

Do you really want to force yourself to believe that tale, Tala Graystone?

An ache brought Tala's hand to her throat, and a mirror throb, lighter but there, radiated from her right hip out across her chest and legs.

"She was in the mouth of a shark." Rowan's voice was flat, carefully devoid of all the fear closing Tala's throat. "Limp, bleeding, while two other sharks were closing in for a fight."

Is that true? Gripping the pillow tighter, Tala squeezed her eyes shut as the feel of water flooded her senses and she fought to remember, to strip truth from panic.

Slowly, the memories flowed, then rushed to her. The water was cold. She'd been swimming fast. She was tired but couldn't rest. There were sharks behind, coral, a foiled strike, a shark she was chasing. And then . . .

Victory and a foolish whale? Or—

Tala drew in a sharp breath.

Then there was a surprising lunge to her unprotected hip. Shark's teeth, row upon row of them, crunching down. Pain, darkness, dreams, and, finally, voices.

Her body is broken.

No, you can turn her back! Back human—you can rebuild her bones in the transformation.

I'm sorry, dear. It's the only way. Don't be too hard on him.

Tala's hands shook, and she forced herself to touch her side, where she'd scraped it on the coral, then her hip, where bones should have cracked. Both spots faintly throbbed at her touch, but it was her throat that burned with agony.

No! It was just the price of the curse. It—

Take courage and face the truth, Tala. You can handle it.

Tala's heaving breaths gradually slowed, her hand slipped from the scale pendant to the covers, and Tala mouthed the truth she couldn't speak but couldn't deny any longer.

Tala the mermaid was dead, and had been before the spell.

Lady Octavia had found in Rowan's unsuspecting error a way to save her life. And she'd repaid them with cruelty.

Not for the first time, Tala fell asleep with the feel of salty water on her face, only this time it was tears and not the sea against her skin.

CHAPTER 14

"Well, off to bed now, you two. For I am off to hunt sunken treasure." Rowan was back in his soggy trousers and shirtsleeves, waves not yet warmed by the still-sleeping sun lapping at his ankles. Spear in hand, he gave his brother and Lily, who'd been his companions all night, a false bright smile and took another step into the sea.

The brisk morning wind and cold water were starting to make him shiver, but the bursting feeling building along his sides and back was of greater concern at the moment. He'd told them everything Lady Octavia had told him and everything that had helped him in his own transformation. He couldn't help Tala directly, but there were still a couple of things he could do for her, and he'd do those.

"Crystim will be at large, on the sea maybe, hunting you." Max set his jaw in that mulish way of his and tugged at the floppy brown cap he always wore now. Rowan was beginning to get a suspicion about that unfashionable thing. He just couldn't say if it was good or bad. "It's too dangerous to go there. Talk to the guides about the best places to find us after tonight."

"I'm not going to reveal myself to him." Rowan took another step, his whole body shivering from the cold and the transformation creeping over him. Unless he wanted to be a beached whale, he needed to hurry on out.

"Tala will come round, Rowan," Lily said quietly as she stood beside Max, tightening the blanket around her shoulders. "She lost her home once when her parents died. Is it any wonder she's clinging so tightly to it now?"

No. The weight of a thousand seas crashed back on Rowan, guilt and shame and excoriations for his blindness. *How could you have done that? Why didn't you realize? Who will ever trust you now? The most beautiful and brave woman you've ever met can't even stand to look at you. You're a failure. You didn't save her life—you murdered it!*

Rowan shook his head, sending the lies flying, and took another step into the waves. They reached his thighs now. *I've asked the Most High for forgiveness, her for forgiveness. My guilt is gone. The true guilt is gone.* He repeated the phrase so hard to believe sometimes. *I won't be dragged down by guilt feelings. Not this time.*

"The point," Max said with a growl, "is that you saved her life, and you have no reason to run away."

That bursting feeling spreading from his scalp to his toes said otherwise. "I'll be okay, Max. *You'll* be okay."

His little brother glowered at him, his hand going to that hat again as his mouth opened.

"Don't make me take that hat, Max."

Max's eyes widened, and Rowan huffed. Just as he thought. That uncanny ability of his and Beau's to find Max in the evenings had to be magic. Their love was strong, but love wasn't a compass. He'd have to ask Lady Octavia where his fool of a little brother had likely stolen it.

"I'm still hoping Lady Violetta shows up with a plan!" Max shouted as Rowan pushed farther into the water now up to his chest.

"Maybe she'll measure out a new hat for you."

"Rowan, this is serious!"

"Believe me, I know." A ripple ran through Rowan's body, the spear disappeared, and he pounded through the waves and dove off the shelf into the deeper water. With a sharp, painful twist, his body expanded and lengthened, his vision and other senses shifted, and he swam away as a whale.

It wasn't far offshore that the sharks started crowding around. They mostly ignored him, but he didn't like that there were so many in the Birney waters, and that they were more aggressive toward humans, boats, and merfolk than typical.

However, despite what his siblings might think, he was not completely useless as a whale. Swim time was excellent thinking time. If his little brother had gotten hold of a magic cap—quite possibly from their enchantress stepmother's hoard—it was likely that the mage or the merman had something similar. Only this artifact, instead of drawing family together, drew sharks and made them more aggressive. And Rowan had an inkling of what it was.

Setting his course for Birney's border with Litvania, Rowan ate his fill of krill as he swam and prayed his hunch was right.

And that being right wouldn't be all wrong for him. For once, he wished he were a narwhale or maybe one of those toothed whales that could eat sharks.

Around midday, Rowan floated lazily over a rock ledge bursting with sea life: corals, anemones, fish, sea horses, and other magnificent creatures. That life puttered out along a narrow strip of rock jutting farther into the sea. Just beyond the last of the coral outcrops rested a plain, open wooden chest with an alluring gold-and-ruby necklace spilling from it. The magic of it vibrated his curse.

Still there, I see.

Three great white sharks circled above it like long, white watchdogs.

Also still there, I see.

Continuing his cruising swim, Rowan searched for any sign of wrecks or any other reason for such a treasure to be sitting, undisturbed by barnacles or men, at the not-quite-bottom-of-the-sea.

When his search returned nothing but an ever-growing suspicion this was the work of Crystim, Rowan very much lamented whales couldn't smirk.

He did not lament that blue whales were larger than sharks. How well they fought, however, was something he was about to find out.

৩৯৯

Rowan was bleeding on his side and thigh when Max pulled him to shore that night. The three brave guards who'd followed him out attacked with spears and arrows the stubborn sharks still after him.

"Lily! Lady Violetta!" Max wrapped an arm around Rowan's waist and towed him toward the blessedly warm fire, repeating his night-shattering cry. The spear, as it tended to, appeared in his hand as he touched shore, and he used it like a staff to aid his steps.

Rowan grunted as Max lowered him to the blanket already splattered with dripped blood. Blasted sharks. They were tenacious, he would give them that. The small chest, tucked between his arm and gashed side, tumbled onto the sand, and he pressed his hand to his side, his fingers soon slick with blood. He must have opened the wound again as he swam the final stretch. He sucked in a breath against the pain and lay back in the sand, his eyes starting to close of their own accord. *You made it, Rowan. You can rest now. Rest.* The word had a heavenly sound to it.

"Don't, Rowan. Keep your eyes open." Max's commanding voice could rouse effort, but not success. He was so tired, so cold.

A canteen shoved into his empty hand and a woman's gasp did draw his eyes, begrudgingly, up, and he saw Lily spin away, calling for a medical kit.

"Rowan," Max warned, but it was the sound of a dagger unsheathing that had Rowan opening eyes he hadn't realized he'd closed again. Max was cutting his pant leg above the wound.

Good little brother. He and Lily would take care of everything.

Rowan began to drift toward dreams again.

"Rowan." A shake to his shoulders had his eyelids bouncing. "Lady Violetta is here."

The enchantress? Rowan jerked and fully woke at a flash of light just in front of him. Temporarily blinded, he could only follow the swish of skirts and the sweet smell of perfume as the most fashionable—and the most underrated when it came to cunning—enchantress glided up to him.

He blinked away the last of the black blobs from his vision to find Lady Violetta frowning down at him and tucking her wand into her belt, an act as incongruous as her outfit. Supple leather boots tied over chestnut brown pantaloons under a sapphire blue skirt split into sections to aid movement, a matching corset over a white blouse, a tricorne hat with a white plume, and a wide leather belt bearing a sword, dagger, spyglass, and a pouch for sundry items. A piece of eight, perhaps?

He arched an eyebrow. Lady Violetta, the most refined of all enchantresses, looked like a pirate queen—a beautiful and elegant pirate queen, but still a pirate queen. Why not some royal at a ball, with a violet gown as large as a doorway, as normal?

Pain shot through his leg, and he dragged his gaze from Lady Violetta to see Max pressing what was left of his pant leg over a gash. Thankfully, the transformation had turned multiple shark bites into two stitchable wounds on his side and leg. Which Lily and Max were now staring at like children faced with an unexpected algebra quiz.

Heaven help him, he was going to have to stitch himself up.

"Prince Rowan," Lady Violetta chided gently, pulling his gaze back up. "We'll discuss how you came by that chest later, and why you look like a poor castaway, but for now, might I be allowed to tend your wounds?" Her expression turned unusually serious, and white gloves materialized around her hands and a white coat around the pirate costume. "There is only so much I can do for another mage's fairy godchildren, you know, without stepping on toes and rules, but I *can* respond to injuries."

Rowan nodded dumbly. Lady Violetta smiled reassuringly and took the medical kit from a stunned Lily's hands. "Prince Max, dear, will you divest your brother of what remains of his shirt? And Princess Lily, perhaps you could ensure Lady Tala and the guards are comfortable? Space and light are essential in these matters, and I wouldn't want a crowd."

Rowan flinched. Little need for that. Tala wouldn't be anywhere around with him here.

CHAPTER 15

"Tala hasn't communicated much all day." Lily and Max shared a worried look. "I'll speak with her and the guards about staying away though." Lily quickly left, and Max helped Rowan out of his shirt.

"Now, let's see," Lady Violetta said as she bent over his leg. "Wounds given by fae monsters are a little different, but don't let that worry you."

Rowan might have fretted anyway, but at a touch of Lady Violetta's hand to his wrist, his pain vanished. The usual first-step implements in these matters—and he had some experience in being stitched up—appeared in a gleaming tray beside her, and he decided the enchantress was more than a fashion plate.

Max, after assuring himself Lady Violetta wasn't going to injure him further, washed Rowan's blood from the chest and opened it. In it was a collar-like, flat gold necklace covered with rose-cut diamonds, with seven rubies like drops of blood draping from it.

Max gave Rowan an incredulous *You risked your life for a ruby necklace?* look.

Hardly.

84

Lady Violetta paused her stitching to raise her eyebrows at the necklace, and maybe it was the pain killer, but Rowan fancied she was impressed.

"Considering what dress might show it off best?" he asked with a lopsided smile, his chest expanding just a bit. He had a faint suspicion the pain relief was the tongue-loosening kind, but he didn't care at the moment.

"When you get into scrapes, Prince Rowan, you at least make them profitable," she said wryly as she shooed Max away and returned to her work. "Is that necklace what I think it is?" She flicked a glance at his injured side, the result of shark teeth.

His stomach tightened as he remembered the sharks attacking him. Attacking Tala.

"It's a necklace of blood," he spat. "I found it by a coral reef at the border of the kingdoms, guarded by sharks." She touched a finger to his wrist again, and though there was no magic to it, the gesture reminded him to calm. He drew in a long breath and let it out in a rush. "I don't think Birney and the merfolk will need to worry about the sharks anymore than usual now."

She *hmm*ed and took another neat stitch, and he was grateful she hadn't contradicted him. "What do you think of my attire, Prince Rowan?" she asked after she'd moved on to his side.

He turned his head to study her, one eyebrow arching at the odd question. Though why the oddities of enchantresses should still surprise was beyond him. "It's a very handsome outfit, but it does not seem much like you."

Lady Violetta chuckled, and it was an enchanting sound. *What would Tala's laugh sound like? Has it been ruined forever?* "It's not for me, dear boy. It's for Lady Octavia."

The words hit him like the keel of a ship. What had he done now? Lady Violetta was a high-ranking enchantress, and the Enchanters Council and Lady Octavia were not on good terms. Had she any plans to force his aunt to Mage Isle?

Perhaps understanding his thoughts, Lady Violetta patted his arm comfortingly before continuing her work. "The Council has changed much since Lady Octavia left, and I have a favor to ask of her."

A favor? Why then the sadness to her voice, years of sorrow her youthful face belied? It seemed so foreign to the glittering persona she wore so well.

His stepmother had once told him of a great war among enchanters themselves, one that overthrew many of its leaders, and which was rumored to have fairy godchildren, and one young enchantress, at its heart.

"The dress is a peace offering," Lady Violetta continued. "I believe she has something a godchild of mine could benefit from, if I can figure out how to work it properly. And it is a handsome outfit, as you say, and I do so love designing outfits. This one is easy care, you know. Dries quickly, and has pockets. It's perfect for her."

"I would only add a ring to slip a pistol through on the belt," Rowan found himself saying.

Lady Violetta's brows puckered for a moment before she smiled brightly. "I know just the spot."

Something shifted on the belt, and the polished wooden handle of a pistol appeared above the leather.

"I don't think you're the same size," Rowan blurted in his surprise, and Lady Violetta laughed.

"Don't you worry about that. I'll get her measurements when I take you there."

"Now, Lady Violetta—" Rowan stammered. Lady Violetta may claim the council wasn't a danger to Lady Octavia, but her aunt might not feel the same way about them, especially if they invaded her island.

"Don't you worry, dear. You can't possibly swim back in your condition, and this is something I really must do. She'll understand. I don't believe half the rumors spread about her —most by her own sister when she's in a mood." She took another stitch, lips pursed as she studied her work. "And no woman wants to look like a sack of potatoes. Some just don't know how to look better, or a few cruel comments or untrustworthy men have made them fear their own femininity. No, she needs this dress. Every woman needs a dress that flatters and is comfortable. Mine always achieve both."

Rowan just stared at her as she finished tending his wounds. When her gloves and white coat vanished, Lily and Max wandered over.

"Now, after you've had time to eat," Lady Violetta said brightly, "I will take you to Lady Octavia." She held up a hand as Max sputtered. "Your brother can't be expected to swim there in his current state." She gave Max a firm look, at which he returned a sheepish nod.

I'll find you when the time is right, brother. Don't worry. I have unfinished business with Lady Tala.

☙❧

The camp grew dark around them as the guards not on patrol settled in for the night, leaving Max, Lily, and Lady Violetta his companions for his human hours. Dinner was an awkward affair, as Rowan was the only one who hadn't eaten, and he hated eating alone. Every bite sounded loud in his ears, making him feel more an uncouth bear than a man, and he very much wanted to feel all human when he had the chance. In desperation, he suggested they examine the necklace.

"What will we do with it?" Max, for once, had the hat in his lap, his wild hair revealing where the hat band had been. Lily and Lady Violetta both looked like they were itching to take a pair of scissors to him. *Good luck evading that, brother.*

"Give it to Lady Octavia," Rowan said, as if that had ever

been in question. A sound like the brush of fabric drew his eyes toward the camp, and for a moment, he thought he saw movement in Tala's tent. But she never emerged, and he turned back to his food. *I'll be gone soon, Tala. You can have your freedom then.*

"Everything pertaining to the sea is hers by right," Lady Violetta said. There was something sly in her tone as she continued, "And Prince Rowan would be wise to bring a trade."

His bite of fish arrested halfway to his mouth, Rowan looked askance at the enchantress. "A trade for what?"

"Have you ever seen a glass bottle with a ship inside?"

"Yes, I've made several."

"You drove us mad trying to figure out how they got the ship in the bottle before Father finally told you," Max added helpfully.

Lady Violetta held out her hand, and a glass bottle with a sleek, familiar ship formed inside it, and Rowan had to repeat his earlier admonishment to trust the enchantress to stifle his growing alarm.

"That's Lady Octavia's ship," Max exclaimed.

"Yes." As Lady Violetta studied the bottle, waves began to crash against the ship's sides, wind billowed the sails, and the ship cut cleanly through the water. She glanced toward the horizon, where dark clouds gathered. "Whalers, I believe, tie their quarry alongside the ship, taking what they want of it while the poor creature is in tow."

Rowan nodded affirmation. He did not think it wise to mention how close he'd come to that same fate a time or two.

"It occurred to me that with the right vessel and a magical artifact or two, that a whale tied to a ship with a trustworthy captain might, at the same time, also be with the ship in a glass bottle. Though *I* do not have the magic to achieve it, one could even swap his days and nights. He would be free to say, join a quest for a crystal ball during the day and sleep in the ocean under the stars at night, safe with the ship."

Rowan's gaze shot to the glass bottle, and for one beautiful moment, night seemed as bright and full of promise as day, but that silent tent behind him rolled the darkened sky back into its place, shadowing even moon and stars.

"That's an admirable idea, Lady Violetta, and we might use a modified plan to keep me with Lady Octavia and so safe as a whale, but I should not return here for a time." There must have been a sense of finality to his tone, for no one said a thing as he finished eating and put away his plate. "Are you ready to go?" he asked.

"Yes, dear," Lady Violetta said quietly, that sadness back in her voice. She set the glass bottle on the sand with a silent, meaningful look at him. Rowan ignored it, set his teeth, and stood. The pain relief, like his leg, was holding, but just barely.

He nodded to Max and cut his gaze over to Lily. "Take care of him for me, won't you? Starting with a hair cut."

Lily blinked at him, her brows drawing together ever so slightly, and he wondered if the light was strong enough for her to lip read. He touched a hand to his hair and nodded to Max.

She smiled, relief sagging her shoulders. "First thing tomorrow."

He returned the smile, tucked the chest under his arm, and held out his hand to Lady Violetta. She took it, and a glow built slowly around them. "Good nigh—"

Beyond the reach of their fire's light, soft footsteps brushed through the sand, awkward in gait but gaining in steadiness and speed. A trim young woman with chestnut hair burst into the light, staggered into Max, swiped the cap from his hand, nearly fell into the sand to retrieve the glass bottle, and flung herself at Rowan.

He caught her to his chest, barely cognizant of the pressure of bottle and cap against his shirt as eyes the color of a forest in summer met his. How could eyes like that belong to the sea? They even had golden flecks of fall amid the green.

And, oddly, something like apology. Lady Tala, proud mermaid ambassador, gestured to the horizon, pressed the bottle and cap to his chest again, and stamped her foot on the sand. "Use them to come back," she mouthed, and then she escaped his arms and fled back to her tent, wobbly on human legs but running all the same.

As the glow of Lady Violetta's magic engulfed them, a ray of light shone on the horizon, and Rowan decided night hadn't just turned to day, winter had turned to summer, and storm to peace, and peace was a forest green.

CHAPTER 16

No. Absolutely not. Never.

Tala glanced at the stubby little tentacles on her feet humans called toes. At Lily's insistence, she was sitting barefoot on the shore, her feet in the sand. The sun shone brightly overhead, but they were still in camp. Beau, as an eagle, had brought them a message, tied to his leg, that King Basil wanted them to delay progress to the Golden Tower. He and Beau had plans against the spies and soldiers Litvania had sent they didn't want Lily and company involved in, and they wanted Max's trainer to join them. After a few days, they would go on to the Tower and Tala to Litvania, to get Meilani back to the sea, one way or another. So now they had two days without travel for Max to figure out how to fight a bull, for Tala to learn how to be human enough to gain entrance to a ball, and for Rowan to return and regain more of his strength.

Prince Rowan of Danskov. The strange human who'd impetuously gotten a mermaid turned into a human, saving her life. Who'd risked his own life to gain a magical necklace to clear the seas, for the safety of everyone but himself.

Who'd been willing to give up the company of friends and family, of being human during the day, to not cause her pain.

Though her heart, and her throat, still ached, for the first time in days, Tala was able to lift her face to the sun and smile. Whatever happened, she was going to be okay. She would love what she was given and find where she could thrive and be of help. It wouldn't be easy, but as her aunt said, nothing good ever was.

Sun-warmed sea water kissed the tips of her feet, and Tala glanced at the strange things humans had in place of delicate fins. With five, ten stubby, little, moveable tentacles at their end.

No. She was not going to do it. She was not the least curious.

Nonetheless, the biggest tentacle bent, then the next, and so on until Tala was bending and straightening all ten of them. Humans really could wiggle them. She scooted her feet forward into the wet sand, intrigued by the feel of the cool grains on and between them, and kept wiggling them.

"They're called toes."

Sucking in a breath, Tala pulled her knees to her chest and tugged her dress back down to her ankles, though she wished she could wash away into the sea like the foam left by the waves.

With a hesitant smile, Rowan gestured to the spot beside her. Tala gave a stiff nod and turned back to the waves. *Courage, Tala. You told him to return.*

Some warning of that event would have been nice though.

With a half-stifled groan, Rowan lowered himself to the sand. She could see the bulge under his pant leg from the bandage. How was he healing?

"Max's cap is really for taking you wherever you wish to go," he said. "For him, his wish for family brought us back to him. Now, it will let me return to Lady Octavia's ship at night." He gave a lopsided smile. "I'll miss campfires, but I'm happy to see the sun again."

Not sure what to say even if she could speak, she nodded and watched the waves with him. When he finally shifted, he didn't rise to leave but reached to his other side. He turned back with the art chest in his hands and gave her that grin again. "I know it's tempting, but I'd appreciate it if you didn't throw it at me, at least not until my other injuries heal."

Her cheeks coloring, Tala huffed and took the chest. She ran her fingers over it, admiring how the sunlight played in the jewels ornamenting it. They were different somehow, perhaps even more beautiful in the sunlight. She quickly opened it and shifted through its contents, ascertaining that it was as she'd left it, only with the addition of two painted oyster shells. Each held a message from her aunt and uncle, and she put those away for when she was alone.

"We thought you could draw out your story to give to Princess Meilani," Rowan began. "Hopefully she'll listen to you and get away from Malosi."

Draw? Tala perked up, ideas already sprouting in her mind.

Rowan shifted as if he were about to rise. "I'll let you get back to learning about toes now."

She shot him a look that faltered at his cocky grin.

"Speaking of toes, Rowan," Max called out. "You should teach her 'The Little Piggy' story. Lily assures me she loves learning human stories."

That was true, but the alarm flashing in Rowan's eyes suddenly made her desire to be alone subordinate to curiosity. She raised her eyebrows in question. "Story?" she mouthed. "If you don't mind."

"Ah . . ."

"Please do, Prince Rowan," Lily called out from her seat in the shade beside Max. "I haven't heard it since I was a little girl."

Rowan looked to Tala, his expression amusingly pleading.

Tala cocked her head and smiled. "Story?"

He blinked at her, his expression almost dazed, then he began with a sigh, "'The Little Piggy,' a nursery rhyme. This—"

"The full version," Max insisted loudly.

Rowan, oddly, looked at her bare feet, his cheeks pinking. He cleared his throat and reached for his big toe. After another great sigh, he pulled back his shoulders and began reciting, hand still on his toe, "This little piggy went to market."

Tala's eyebrows went to her hairline, and he reached for the next toe, moving down the line, jiggling each one as he reached its part of the tale.

"This little piggy stayed home. This little piggy had roast beef. This little piggy had none. This little piggy went . . . *wee, wee, wee*, all the way home."

Tala bit her lip to keep from bursting with laughter as his voice went higher with each *wee*. Big, tough warrior who fought with sharks, indeed.

Fingers still clasping his little toe, Rowan cleared his throat again. "It's for children. I mean something parents tell their children."

As she fought to smooth out her lips, he cleared his throat again and released his toe.

She nodded very seriously, though that mischievous side of herself, which had gotten her in trouble often as a little girl, soon had her signing, "Would you repeat it so I can learn it?"

Rowan frowned, but when she smiled at him, eyes wide in innocent supplication, he blinked and began again.

As soon as he finished his high-pitched *wee, wee, wee* this time though, he began to push up. He didn't get far before grimacing and pausing to take a steadying breath. He gave her an apologetic smile that somehow cut. Was he, with his injuries and the dark circles under his eyes showing how little he'd slept as human or whale for who knew how long, to move while she, with whole legs, stayed?

"If you'll give me a minute," he said, "I'll leave you to your treasure and go rest in the shade."

She started to gather her strewn art supplies. "Wait, Prince Rowan, I can move—"

"Stay right there, yon invalid! And yon artist!" Max jogged over with a wide-brimmed hat, a blanket, and a canteen of water. He settled the hat over Rowan's jet black hair, and as his brother glared at him, tucked the blanket about his waist and placed the canteen beside him. He pulled an amber bottle of medicine from his jacket and buried it to its neck in the sand. "Now, you can both stay here. I'll even bring over the leaf umbrella Lily and I have been working on as soon as it's ready." He pointed with his foot to the buried bottle. "He'll need to take some of that in a couple of hours, Tala."

He was making her responsible for Rowan's medicine? Max dashed off before either could say anything. While she was not running from the human's presence, Tala had no intention of spending all day with him. She started to protest, but a remembrance of his earlier grimace made her plans stumble over themselves.

A flabbergasted Rowan turned her way, an apology in his expression. Pasting on a kind smile, Tala gestured for him to lie down. He'd only fall asleep, and that hardly counted as being near, did it?

He gave her a grateful smile that somehow made hers a little less forced, and irritated her for that. He settled back in the sand, tipped the hat over his face, and was soon fast asleep.

Tala took up her art chest, and, ready to ignore Rowan, she began sketching out her story on the curved underside of oyster shells.

And yet, the prince's soft breathing was somehow difficult to ignore, and when the wind blew his hat away, and he didn't stir, Tala had to chase it down. When sea gulls pecked at his blanket, she had to shoo them away. When the sun grew warm, she had to wake him to give him his medicine and ensure he drank before he drifted to sleep again.

Then there was the waking for dinner, him trying to help her up and both nearly tumbling to the ground on their weak legs, the conversation Lily insisted she join by lip reading everything she mouthed, and him smiling softly every time he looked at her.

And so it was, by the time evening flowed into the cove and Rowan took up the spear, glass bottle, and cap, as lightning flashed around the model ship and he disappeared, Tala had forgotten she intended to avoid him.

CHAPTER 17

Tala woke the next morning when Lily poked her with the butt of a pair of scissors.

"I've been waiting for this since the week after Max showed up," Lily said cheerfully as she raised the scissors. "Last time I tried to convince him to get his hair cut, your uncle showed up unexpectedly with the plan to make you ambassador, and we had to get things ready for you." Her brows furrowed, and she gave the scissors a worried look, which made her cursed face especially horrid to look at. "Have you ever cut a man's hair?"

Tala, still groggy, shook her head and sat up.

"Hmm. Oh well. I'll just trim it and leave it long enough for someone else to fix if things go wrong. But at least it won't be so wild," Lily decided happily.

"Or get in his eyes when he fights the bull," Tala mouthed, being sure to face Lily.

"Good point. I'll mention that if he balks."

In a few moments, Lily and Tala, dressed and hair plaited, left the tent, Lily intent on cornering Max and Tala intent on not being unofficially assigned babysitting duty for Rowan.

Though she did need to make sure he took his medicine this morning.

That thought in mind, they followed the sound of movement away from the campfire to outside the ring of tents, toward the path to the cliff base.

Just outside camp, Max was crouched, sword drawn, facing off with a bear of a man with swarthy skin, a thick black beard, and a strange tattoo on his neck.

"How did you get past the guards?" Max growled at the intruder. "What did you do to them?"

The stranger gave a dark chuckle. "I stole quietly past them."

Lily gasped and snagged Tala's arm. The two eased back into the trees beside the trail.

"I doubt that." Max used his sword to point to the man's neck. "That's a Litvanian prisoner tattoo on your neck."

"You have sharper eyes than they, I'll give you that, prince."

Wishing she had a pair of scissors or a sword herself, Tala looked around the camp. Where were the other guards? She didn't even see Rowan! If he'd returned, he was probably in the tent asleep. *Wake up and do something!*

"What is it that you want?" Max asked, inching nearer the man.

The stranger lunged forward, then back as Max parried and produced a dagger from somewhere, nearly gutting the man with it.

The intruder chuckled as he took another step away and crouched again. "I didn't take you for the kind of man who stabbed first and asked questions later."

"I'm not." Max shifted to keep himself between the intruder and the girls. "I *am* asking questions."

Tala tugged on Lily's sleeve to get her attention. "What should we do?"

Lily shook her head, eyebrows pinched as she turned to stare at the big man.

"Then maybe not the right ones."

Max's jaw tensed, but he asked, "How did you end up in Litvania's prison then?"

"That's better, boy." A hardness etched deeper lines in his sun-weathered face. "I was tired of torturing and killing animals for sport in the nobles' arena, and training them for it. We freed the poor creatures, but I was caught and sentenced for costing the nobles money."

"You let a lot of trained killers loose!" Max gave a wild look around, as if expecting vicious animals to jump from the forest onto them.

"The ones who make them fight deserve what they get." The man grinned wickedly, showing off even, white teeth.

Tala's hand reached for her aching throat. Teeth were dangerous. And as much as Tala hated the thought of any creatures being used in blood sports, what if they'd followed the man and were even now stalking the camp? Was this man like a shark of the land? "Lily—"

"Thwarted again!" Lily threw down the scissors with a huff and crossed her arms.

Max, for a split second, turned her way, then blocked a blow from the stranger before quickly backing away again.

"You distract too easily, prince. But at least you recover quickly."

Tala tugged at Lily's arm. They needed to do something! Find the traitorous guards' weapons or wake the sleeping Rowan. Even if he was injured, his presence ought to be a threat! Any man who fought sharks and won was no coward.

Lily brushed her off again, picked up the scissors, and marched from their shadowed shelter, straight for the crouching pair. That wasn't what Tala had in mind! "That's enough, Luska," Lily scolded, scowling and shaking her scissors at the man. "We haven't even eaten breakfast yet."

To Tala's shock, this Luska laughed, not cruelly, but in fond amusement. He sheathed his sword and bowed to Lily and to Max, who was gaping at him.

"Lily!" Max warned, trying to block her way.

"He's one of the kennel keepers and combat trainers for my father." Lily stopped beside Max and gestured to a hat tucked into the man's belt. It bore Birney's colors. "He's been gone for a while, and shaved his head. I almost didn't recognize him. Those animals he released are in a preserve being cared for. After he escaped prison, some of my grandfather's friends helped him flee Litvania." Lily motioned from Max to the trainer. "Prince Maximillian, this is Luska. Lady Tala, Luska."

"Well met, Your Highness." Luska bowed gracefully for one so fierce in appearance. "My apologies for distressing you. King Basil sent me to teach you how to fight a magical bull. And men, if needed." Max straightened, a tension Tala hadn't noticed falling from his shoulders. Had he been nervous about fighting the bull? Luska smirked. "But first, your breakfast awaits."

"First." Tala jumped at the baritone voice behind her and spun around. Rowan, leaning on a spear she should ask how he came by, his two-day scruff giving him a roguish appearance, winked at her. The gesture did something strange to her insides, and Tala bristled. No human was going to charm her. He returned an amused smirk for her glower.

"First," he repeated when everyone turned to him, including the guards suspiciously present again, "some able-bodied men might want to look into what's just washed ashore."

"A beached whale in need of a shave, perchance?" Tala mouthed.

His brows drew together in question as he studied her lips, and it was Tala's turn to smirk.

Lily jogged to them. "She said a beached whale in need of

a shave washed up. But we'll let you keep the beard if you'll convince Max to cut his hair."

"Lily!" What was the point of not having a voice if she couldn't say anything she wanted! Before she could complain further, her friend dragged her away down the path, leaving Rowan to hobble along behind alone. She poked Lily and mimed drinking from a small bottle.

"Tala wants to know if you took your medicine this morning, Rowan. She's concerned for you," Lily called back, and Tala very seriously considered how international relations would fare if she tripped the princess of Birney.

They reached the shore just after Max and a couple guards ringed a wooden travel chest stuck in the sand, its lid conveniently ajar, waves slapping its iron-banded bottom.

"There are little flowers worked into the bands." Max ran his fingers over the metal strips securing the wood. He glanced at the unlocked lid with suspicion.

Tala scanned the shore for wrecks but saw nothing. Objects that heavy didn't wash to land on calm seas. Was this some trick of Malosi's?

"When we visited Lady Octavia," Rowan huffed out as he limped past the campfire toward them, "Lady Violetta made a number of comments about being unable to provide further *direct* help for us."

Max studied the trunk a moment longer, ran his finger over the flower images, and flipped open the lid.

Fabric?

"Now that is treasure indeed." Lily waded into the water as Max straightened away from the trunk to scratch his head in confusion. She pulled out a simple yet elegant gown the color of her true eyes and held it tightly to her chest, like it were a thing beloved. She replaced it to retrieve a folded man's suit, the bundle tied with an orange ribbon.

"Fireproof," Lily read the tag, then passed it off to Max. "The fiery bird with the flaming egg comes after the bull."

The next bundle was another suit. "Waterproof and shark-teeth resistant." She tossed that to a guard to take to Rowan, who'd managed to get as far as the wet sand, beside Tala.

Lily paused and glanced at Tala before reaching deeper into the trunk to pull out another gown. Tala's breath caught. "Will not sink," Lily read, her gaze capturing Tala's. Holding the gown by the shoulders, she let its bodice and full skirt cascade down in front of her, encouraging the sunlight to show off the gown's sapphire blue fabric.

It was the color and even the iridescence of Tala's scales.

It looked like *her*.

As Tala blinked away tears, she felt more than saw Rowan look down at her. "I think," he said, a bittersweetness to his voice she well understood, "that color would look exceptionally lovely on you, Lady Tala."

CHAPTER 18

Heaven help him, but Rowan wanted to convince Lady Tala to stay human. In only a few days, he'd gone from desperate to find a way to undo "the curse" and send her home, to wanting to help her bear it, to wanting to make her want it.

Lily had commanded everyone to change into their new outfits, and now they were admiring them and each others' by the shore. Tala was actually smiling as she looked down at her dress, a small restoration of what she'd lost. Rowan had been dazzled by smiles before, and learned his lesson, but when he saw hers, he couldn't help but remember how she'd run after him and flung herself and the bottle into his arms to make sure he came back—because she'd forgiven him. And when he'd watched her at her art during his few waking moments the previous day, he'd gotten the sense they appreciated similar things and could be friends, if she'd let him.

"Human ladies tend to twirl in front of a mirror when they get a new dress," he found himself saying as she continued to study the gown. Tala's eyebrows drew together in question. "Helps them see the back, and I think they just like the motion. Makes them think of dancing, and they all like dancing."

"Like this." Lily twirled, her skirts flaring out around her. It was a pretty motion.

Tala watched, then looked down at her feet, began to twirl, and teetered like a spinning top losing its momentum.

"Whoa there." Rowan lunged forward on his good leg and caught her arm as she grabbed his sleeve. "You're a lot taller than a toddler. We don't want you falling." He felt like spinning himself when she didn't immediately jerk away, chin in the air and fire in her eyes. She kept hold of his sleeve instead and frowned down at her feet, which were at an awkward angle.

She carefully untangled her feet and planted them firmly on the sand before releasing him.

"You're not going to let a little human thing like twirling get the better of you?" he asked, a challenge in his tone. Tala narrowed her eyes at him. A competitive spirit, hmm? That could be useful. "Lily will be happy to repeat the motion more slowly, won't you, Lily?"

"Of course." A scheming look in her eyes he didn't mind at all, Lily lifted the hem of her skirt, planted one foot, and began to spin. "Now, there are a couple of ways to twirl," she began. "One where you plant one foot and spin, and another where you move both feet. The former is a bit more dizzying but the footwork is simpler, so start with that. If you feel like you're going to fall, Rowan would be happy to be your strong anchor."

Tala did shoot him and Lily a suspicious glare then. He gave her his most roguish grin, then thrust his spear deep into the sand, nodded to it, and took a step back. There was no way he was going to scare her away.

And when he caught her blushing and glancing between him and the spear, something grateful in her expression, he knew there was no way he was going to run away either.

Lady Tala of Crestfall was going to know him and the human world enough to have a choice about which world she most wanted to belong to before they found the crystal ball.

❀❀❀

Tala had her spinning lessons, and Max had his bullfighting lessons.

Max managed to only get gored by Luska's imaginary bull twice, and Rowan got to catch Tala once, and got to see her beam as she mastered the very human art of spinning to show off a dress.

He also received Max's glower and Luska's knowing look for ignoring their fights, but he wasn't the least bothered.

"Your brother is a fast learner, Prince Rowan," Luska said as they ate dinner together. "And you a fast healer." He looked Rowan up and down, brow arched in question. Rowan's side and leg were still sore, and he limped, but he felt two weeks along in his healing rather than two days.

"I really was injured. I don't know what Lady Octavia and Lady Violetta did to me, but it worked exceptionally well."

"Hmm," Luska said, as if not fully satisfied but not finding the question worth his effort at the moment. The "trainer" was far more than he seemed, Rowan suspected, but as with Lady Octavia and Lady Violetta, he had more concerns than the mystery of them at present. He would content himself with gratitude.

"Well," Luska continued, angling away from Rowan, as he often did, "we will leave for the Tower tomorrow and practice in the evenings. We'll have short riding days so you'll have time to eat before returning to the sea and for more practice time for Prince Max. And as I have much to tell him, he and I will ride together, and you'll ride alongside Lady Tala and help her with her human and horseback riding lessons. Prince Max says she is not a skilled land horse rider yet, and the trails through the mountains are taxing. Think you can manage that?"

Grinning like a madman, Rowan spun around, yelling when he spotted Tala walking along the shore with Lily. "You hear that, Lady Tala? You're stuck with me again tomorrow."

She paused to glare with practiced disdain at Luska and walked on, which Rowan chose to take as approval of the arrangement.

CHAPTER 19

While Tala contemplated breaking the glass bottle Luska insisted she take charge of for a time, she restrained herself and merely glowered at Rowan as he appeared the next morning, a merking's spear in his hand and far too bright a smile on his unshaven, roguishly handsome face.

"I made it back, I see, so I guess you don't hate me any longer?" He gestured for the bottle, and when she gave it to him, he placed it in a padded box in a leather bag slung about his chest.

"Don't tempt me," she mouthed. "I do this for Max's sake alone, pirate-face."

The smile only grew more cocky. "You're in luck, you know, Lady Tala. Lady Octavia and Lady Violetta gave me a lip-reading spell!"

They did *what*? Tala threw her hands up in exasperation and turned away. She'd not made it three feet toward her mare when her movement was arrested by a light touch to her arm.

"As you're learning not just how to be a human," Rowan

said as he tucked her arm through his, "but how to be a human lady attending a ball—"

She freed herself and crossed her arms over her chest.

Amusement making his dark eyes sparkle and Tala regret not breaking that bottle, he held out his elbow in a strange gesture of offering. "You must learn to walk with a gentleman. Arms linked." He gave her a look of challenge. "Unless you're afraid of me?"

"You are far too smug, Rowan of Danskov." Tala held out her hand.

Rowan's lips curled ever so slightly. "Are we making a pact, Lady Tala? Striking a deal? Shaking hands as a show of forgiveness? Belatedly greeting one another? . . . Having a romantic stroll?"

Tala frowned at him. "What do you mean? You need my hand to link arms, do you not?"

"No." He wiggled his open elbow. "I offer a spot, and *you* accept by placing your hand on my arm. But don't worry. We have a saying that you should 'keep your friends close and your enemies closer,' so I won't take it amiss if you sidle up next to me." He waggled his eyebrows, and she rolled her eyes and slipped her hand into the crook of his elbow. He adjusted the position of her hand and scooted closer to her, letting her arm relax against his.

"Are you ready?" he asked, leaning awkwardly toward her.

"I think I can manage the five feet to the horses," she replied tartly, leaning away from him.

"Now who's smug?" He led her to the horse and helped her up, giving constant direction on whatever topics came to mind: when to take and not take a gentleman's arm, what offering a hand meant, how to mount a horse, and so on.

They found their place near the rear of the caravan, a few guards behind them. Soon, they left the cove on a gently sloping road and entered a forest, following a trail that led over roots and up and down little shallow streams, through a meadow, and over the occasional fallen log. Rowan kept close beside her, a fact she didn't want to admit was comforting, especially when her mare stopped in a flowing stream and began to lie down.

When he wasn't teaching or correcting her regarding horses, Rowan was pointing out plants and flowers, shadows and light, in the way of an artist. He saw beauty here the same way she saw it in the ocean, and, especially under his tutelage, now in the human world. She wanted to capture each scene, the details and colors of a leaf he tore from a tree for her, the beams of light falling through the trees he made sure she saw. She wanted to learn to paint on canvases she designed and built, as humans did, rather than be confined to the size and shape of the shells and driftwood she could find. The strength of the longing, to be a part of this human world, made her shift uncomfortably in her saddle and her mood to sour.

"You're taking advantage of the fact I can't speak," she muttered as Rowan, with an amused rebuke, corrected her hold on the reins a third time a couple of hours into the ride. If she could ask questions, she wouldn't need so much correcting!

"Nonsense. I always watch to see if you have something to say."

When she started and turned fully to him, he winked, and she realized not only that the gesture caused an unfortunate dance of sea horses in her stomach, that his awkward angle of riding was purposeful—so he could read her lips. He *wanted* to be able to listen to her, and she hadn't even considered the possibility of talking to him. When had Tala, the polite and considerate mermaid ambassador, become so critical and self-focused?

"Sorry," she mouthed, and he grinned at her, eyes twinkling.

"Are you apologizing to me or the horse?"

Those sea horses started racing about again, and she felt the sudden need to get away, politeness be hanged. "Both. I tire of this plodding pace. Excuse me." She fixed her hold on the reins and adjusted her posture as he'd told her multiple times already, and urged the horse into greater speed. Which soon turned into an unpleasant, unsettling, and decidedly undesirable bounce across a broad, sunny meadow.

"Rowan!" she cried as she hit the saddle hard, the horse veering off into the meadow rather than following the others along its edge.

"You wanted to go faster," he said, chuckling, as he came alongside her again, seemingly not the least concerned about the unnatural motion of the horse. "Should I rein you in from this dangerous pace and sweep you onto my horse as a true hero would . . . or teach you how to handle a canter before you accidently send your mare into a gallop?"

"Teach!" she exclaimed as she grabbed hold of the horse's mane for dear life.

"That's my girl." He leaned over enough to comfortingly pat the mare's shoulder. As if *she* needed it!

"I'm not your girl!" But even as she protested, Tala had the terrifying feeling it could, one day, be true, and only the thought that she would need Rowan to save her from whatever "gallop" was kept her from kicking her mare's sides again.

"It's just an expression of approval from a mentor, Tala." He touched her back, and she straightened automatically. "That's right," he said, his voice soothing. "Keep your shoulders over your hips, and let your hips swish over the saddle back to front with the horse's motion. You bouncing up and down on her back is just as hard for her as for you."

Sorry, horse. "Swish?"

"Yes. You've swished your tail fins before, I'm sure. Watch the rest of us, our hips in particular."

Feeling as if she were taking her life in her hands, Tala

dared a glance away from the meadow grass to study Rowan beside her and attempted to sweep her hips over the saddle in a similar motion. It took a few tries, but eventually, the ride grew easier, the motion more automatic.

"There you go," Rowan encouraged. "You're a natural."

Tala broke into a smile. "The motion reminds me a bit of how we swim."

"Good. Now let's slow back to a walk. We've a long day of riding."

Remembering what he'd taught her, she eased the horse into a walk, her body losing some of its tension at the easier gait.

"And now what would you like to learn?" Rowan asked as they entered the forest, once again in their place in line. "I don't want to talk your ear off as they say, but we only have so much time before the Tower and Litvania."

Tala nodded in understanding, then, turning toward Rowan so he could see her lips more easily, she began asking her questions.

◈✦◈

Sore did not fully describe how Tala felt by the end of the day, and yet she was not as weary as she'd expected. A whisper from her heart suggested it was the company that made the long day somehow bright, but she buried that thought alongside the ones of admiration for the human world.

Instead, as the men set up camp, she enjoyed grooming her horse alongside Lily, then getting a campfire cooking lesson from Max and Rowan, and at dinner, talking with her companions about the day and about Luska's and Max's ideas on fighting the bull and how to best chase a magical bird. Finally, their evening together came to a close. As

Rowan and Max strode away with the glass bottle and cap toward their tent, Lily turned to Tala with a weary smile.

"I don't know about you, but I would love a good long soak. One of the guards said there's a hot spring just over that rise." She nodded across their little woodland camp toward a raised strip of forest. "Care to join me for a private bath?"

A memory of water burning her eyes and lungs caused Tala's throat to close, her heart to pound. "You go ahead," she blurted. "I'll . . . clean up briefly in the morning."

Lily cocked her head to study her. "Are you okay? The guards will make sure we have our privacy."

"I'm fine. I need to make progress on my designs, and my throat aches." Tala forced a smile. "Enjoy your bath." She hurried away, ignoring Lily's surprise and Max's and Rowan's glance at her.

With her art chest in her lap, her tools in her hands, she tried not to think about her beloved ocean trying to destroy her. Soon though, it was Rowan's teasing offer to sweep her onto his horse, the way his eyes lit with friendly mischief and darkened with concern, that consumed her thoughts and ate away bit by bit at the future she thought she wanted.

CHAPTER 20

The next few days continued much the same, though surprisingly enjoyable friendly conversations replaced many of the lectures. There were still those, however. A repeat on cantering, a lesson on galloping, one on how a human jumps that elicited many laughs, more walks with a gentleman.

How to dance with a gentleman.

Tala and her uncle had once attended a ball in those horrid contraptions, and she remembered very much wanting to join the dancing. In that moment, the beauty of human clothes and jewels had made up for the lack of scales. The fluidity with which the humans danced replaced their usual bland walking pattern with something approaching the grace of swimming. It made her want to move, but the music fit human movement more than what she could do as a mermaid in the sea, much less in a contraption. It was made for legs and a floor.

A forest floor of leaves, wildflowers, and roots probably wasn't typical for dancing, but no complaints would be allowed, and she found herself not wanting to make any as they gathered for lessons. When Luska declared that Rowan, while better, wasn't up to dancing yet, however, she wasn't sure she was disappointed or relieved.

As Max played on a violin that had conveniently been at the bottom of the washed-ashore trunk, Luska took it upon himself to be Tala's partner while Lily gave instructions. Who knew counting was so important to dancing!

"Will you be able to dance at the ball?" Tala found herself asking Rowan as he, leaning on that merking spear, watched her struggle through the waltz's box step.

Pleased surprise shone in his eyes before he gave her a soft smile. "Balls are usually after-dark affairs, and they don't invite whales."

"Oh." Even Tala could hear the disappointment in her voice.

A very masculine smugness tilted Rowan's lips before Luska called her attention away. She'd forgotten the rise and fall pattern again—she wasn't used to that motion, and it tired her legs.

"Do we need lessons on standing on tiptoes to build your muscles?" Luska asked, one eyebrow arched.

"No," Tala said quickly.

"Hmm. Stop looking at your feet."

Tala, guilty as an octopus who'd just inked, raised her gaze to Luska instead, for all of three sweeping box steps around the camp.

"Don't count aloud, don't look at your feet, and *don't* look at me," he scolded as Tala's feet stopped moving altogether. There was something odd about Luska, particularly his eyes —like he had a faint gold line through them. She'd long had an odd feeling about him, but this close up . . .

"Are you human?" If he had fae blood in him, then the story Lily had suggested was far from what Luska had really been up to in Litvania, for no regular human prison could hold him.

That gold line glimmered in answer. "Sometimes that's not the whole story, is it, Lady Tala?"

Tala held his gaze long enough to be sure nothing sinister lurked there. Something wild and dangerous yes, but not a threat to the good, to her friends. She looked down at her gown-covered legs. *Or even the half of it . . .*

Before she could respond, he started her moving again. "I prefer to keep my secrets, Lady Tala, and share only my expertise. Dancing in this case. Don't look at your feet and don't look at me. Prince Rowan, make yourself useful and keep where Lady Tala can look at you. She won't be dancing with a servant at the ball, after all."

"She won't be able to look away." Rowan winked at her.

She wrinkled her nose at him but then obediently fastened her gaze on him. The music continued, and Tala listened to it and to Lily and Luska but watched Rowan as she urged her spindly human legs to move in rhythm.

"One, two, three. One, two, three, look at me," Rowan urged, and it was with a guilty sort of pleasure that she did. She'd glanced at him many times, but staring was rude even for merfolk. Now she could study him, this human who'd been deemed worthy to hold a King Spear. Whose voice had grown comfortingly familiar. Whose friendship was growing more sure every day. Was all of that in his face? Or was it just a human male face?

At least she could see it all easily now. Rowan had finally shaved, and he and Max both had let Luska cut their hair. With the suit Lady Violetta had gifted him, he looked very much a prince. An undeniably handsome one. There were mermen as or even more handsome—Malosi, for one—but she didn't know any who had such kindness and loyalty and honor to go with it, and as she studied Rowan's face, she found she could see it all there. The combination was almost irresistible. *If only he were a merman.*

If only? You're not a mermaid . . .

There was such unexpected peace in the thought, Tala missed her step and landed on Luska's foot.

"If you're tired," Luska said as she apologized and tried to get back into rhythm, "we can end the lesson for the afternoon."

Tala peeked at Rowan, fearing a return of that masculine smugness, but he only studied her seriously. She nodded to Luska and patted her chest. "I am tired."

"That's enough for today then. You're doing well, so a break won't hurt." He led her back to her "spot along the wall" as a gentleman would. He left her with a bow, soon taking Max and Rowan with him for sparring lessons. As the three strode away, the answer to the question from earlier, of whether she was regretful or relieved Rowan hadn't been well enough to dance, became as clear as still lagoon water.

Tala very much wanted Rowan at the ball.

🕸

The next afternoon, after an early stop to deal with a horse with a sore hoof, Lily and Tala found a couple of promising boulders and took their ease on them.

"My body hurts in places I can't even name." Tala pointed to different areas of her leg, whose muscles were now loudly proclaiming their existence. They'd done a bit more walking than usual, and that uphill, to help the horses.

Lily chuckled, then shook her head in fond exasperation as Max, who was helping Rowan unpack a tent, burst out in song, "Head, shoulders, knees, and toes. And eyes and ears and mouth and nose."

"Max," Lily scolded. "She's not a baby."

"Sorry," Max replied. "I should have known something more advanced was called for." He grinned at Rowan, who threw his arm over his brother's shoulder as the two began singing, with the accompanying motions, "Dem bones dem bones dem dry bones . . . knee bone connected to the thigh bone, thigh bone connected to the hip bone, hip bone connected to the back bone . . . "

Tala bit her lip against a smile but couldn't help but pay attention too.

"Is it helping?" Lily asked, amused, as the brothers continued the song.

Tala poked her sore upper leg. "Thigh. I did not know that."

"I'm not surprised that hurts." Lily touched the back of her lower leg. "Not in the song, but 'calf muscle.' It gets sore often too, especially when going uphill."

"Calf? Like a baby whale? How appropriate it should pain me."

Lily chuckled and pointed past the edge of camp, to a little trail. "There's another hot spring over there. I'm going for a soak later if you want to join. It'll help the soreness."

Water closed in over Tala's head again, setting her lungs afire. "No, thank you," she said quickly. "I'll clean up in the morning. I need to work on the story for Meilani."

Lily eyed her a moment, and Tala got the feeling her refusals were limited before her friend dragged the truth from her.

"Max plays the violin beautifully," Tala said.

A narrow-eyed look warned Tala that Lily knew that tactic. "Yes," Lily said, smiling now. "And when he and Rowan goof off like they're doing now, it makes me miss Lysander. Brothers are special. If that princess of yours hurts him, I'll rip out her hair."

"I'll help," Tala said. So long as they found her before she turned to sea foam, if this Crystim had really used the sea witch's ancient spell. She left Lily to collect her art chest and sit on a boulder out of the way.

She was tapping her shark-tooth stylus against her palm, contemplating how to image Crystim when a familiar, slightly limping gait set her ridiculous heart off-rhythm, in a kind of one-two-three beat that made her want to hum. She looked up, schooling her lips into no more than a friendly smile as Rowan placed himself across from her, his injured leg stretched out.

"All right, spill it, Sardines."

Her stylus stilled mid-air. "I beg your pardon?"

"Is that the wrong pet name? Tuna, Fins? Max said Mackerel made you particularly indignant, so I was saving that one for another time." When she huffed, he smiled, a hint of concern in his eyes that put her on guard. "You're a mermaid at heart, Tala, and yet you've refused a nice, warm soak in the water several nights in a row. Is it because it's fresh water? Your human skin won't shrivel in it, well, not too soon anyway, and hot spring water has lots of minerals, so it's a bit more like sea water. You don't stink, so I know you're not opposed to bathing. Why not enjoy the water?"

"It . . . It's still not seawater," she said more sharply than she meant to, and yet she couldn't force anything more through her aching throat. Her hands twisted in her lap, over the scale-colored dress Lady Violetta had claimed would not sink. It might not, but *she* would.

When Rowan's gazed dropped to her hands, his brow furrowing with concern, she picked up her art chest and began digging through it.

"Would you at least like to see the hot spring? It's a pretty spot, a pool ringed with stone in a little canyon of moss and rock and trees."

She shook her head, still not looking at him. She felt him study her a moment before standing slowly to his feet.

"I'll leave you to your art, but let me know if I can do anything."

She nodded, and he began walking away, pace slow.

You're such a coward, Tala! Tell him.
It's his fault!

That I'm still alive? Yes, it is. And it's his fault the message to Crestfall got through. It's his fault sharks no longer terrorize Birney's waters. It's his fault that, though I miss my old life, I'm growing to like this one.

Tala hastily stood. "Rowan?"

He kept walking, and Tala's heart gave a strange and painful twist. Had she been sharp and rude too many times?

Don't be as dumb as a tuna—he can't see you!

Tala snatched up a rock and cracked it against another. Rowan spun around. She met his gaze. "Rowan?"

"Yes?" That soft smile was back on his face, no anger or irritation suggesting he wanted to be on his way.

Tala's frantic heartbeat began to slow, though it threatened to speed again when she thought about what she had to say. She forced herself to hold his gaze, despite the fear that had to be showing in hers, the shame. "I don't know how to swim as a human."

His eyebrows rose, he muttered something about him being an idiot, then he walked back and offered her his hand. "I can help with that."

CHAPTER 21

"Are Max's pants and witnesses really necessary?" Tala had her blanket wrapped so tightly around her one would think she was afraid of a breeze turning her into a model of a painting titled *Nude Nymph in the Forest*.

"Yes, Tala." Rowan carefully eased himself into the hot spring. The pool was about fifteen feet across, and its rocks were somewhat slick, but the water came up to his waist for most of its width. And the temperature was just below being too hot. It was perfect. "Gowns are too restrictive and heavy when wet to swim in, and yours, according to its label, 'will not sink.' Hardly conducive to teaching someone to float and swim." He waded toward her ledge and waved his hand at her. "Come on."

Eyes going wide, she inched away. Lily, sitting beside her, soaking her feet as Max worked through the forms on a staff Luska had given him, placed a restraining hand on Tala's leg.

"In you go or I shall push you in," Lily declared.

Tala stilled, her shoulders drooped, and she dropped the blanket on Lily's head. As Lily sputtered and threw off the blanket, Rowan made note of the fact women looked oddly terrible and oddly attractive in men's clothing, especially when the waist was cinched tight enough and shirt tucked tight enough to show off a curvy figure. His mermaid was a beauty inside and out, no matter how she felt about legs and a lack of scales. If only he could convince her being human wasn't such a bad thing.

Tala quickly sat, as if attempting to hide her outfit, and scooted to the edge of the ledge, feet dangling in the water. Rowan lifted her into the pool and kept hold of one hand as he led her a few feet away from the ledge. She maintained a death grip on his hand, her other arm wrapped around his, and he had a difficult time being altruistic enough to feel bad about her fear.

"Now that those atrocious legs of yours are hidden from view under the water," he said as he positioned her perpendicular to his chest, "we can start with the first lesson of swimming: knowing your surroundings. Tell me what you see."

She shot him a glare and mimed swimming.

He shook his head. *Not yet.* "I need your pulse to go down, Tala. Tell me what you see. How does this glade please the eye? How does the hot spring feel? How deep is it? Where can you walk and where would be above your head? What dangers might there be and how can you avoid or deal with them?"

She pressed her lips together but then began describing the glade and spring. Her grip slowly loosened, and he began to explain how human swimmers breathe—not in the water, never in the water—and how to float.

By the time he dipped her into the pleasantly hot pool, supporting her as she floated on her back, she'd lost her fear to determination. And when he released her to float on her own, it took her a whole minute to realize and grab for his arm. She began sinking and mouthing cries of alarm and extreme displeasure with him.

As she struggled to get her feet underneath her and stand, and he fought to not be tugged under on accident, and Lily laughed at them both, the twang of bowstrings and cries of soldiers silenced even the glen's birds.

An arrow thunked into the ground a few feet from Lily, and she darted into the woods as Max ran from tree to tree toward their camp and the source of the attack. Rowan, desperately wishing Tala knew how to swim underwater, pushed her toward a rock jutting into the hot spring near the camp side of the pool.

Just before they ducked beneath the moss-draped ledge, an arrow sliced through the water where Rowan had been standing. He caught sight of the fletching as it sank: Litvania's colors.

Crouched side-by-side with water lapping at their chins, they waded until rock met bank, hid themselves in its shadows, and listened. Sound echoed strangely to them between stone and water, but the roars of warriors and screams of horses, the clash of metal and whistle of arrows were strong at their camp. Yet nothing approached.

Should he go after Lily? Sneak to the camp to help Max, Luska, and the guards? His spear and sword were on the other side of the pool though. Where were the soldiers King Basil sent to clear this area near the Tower!

"Tala." Rowan guided her hand from his arm to the bank, letting it stabilize her into the muscle-burning crouch. "I need to check on Lily and get my spear and sword." When she opened her mouth to protest, he shook his head. "I can swim underwater to reach the other side of the pool without being seen. You'll be safe here, and I'll be right back."

Tala studied his face in the shadows, then nodded, so much bravery despite fear in her expression he was tempted to kiss her, but that would hardly leave him clear-headed for sneaking about and fighting. It might also get him slapped.

He scooted out around her before he could do anything foolish, peeked around the ledge, and braced himself for swimming injured. He was about to dive when a hand gripped his sleeve. Tala pulled him back, kissed his cheek, and motioned him away.

Rowan was at the other side of the pool in a thrice, ready to take on the world: traitorous mermen ambassadors, cowardly mages, feisty mermaids, and pretty much anyone else. Instead, he hunkered down near a boulder as a dark-clad man and four riderless horses thundered into camp followed by four mounted Litvanian soldiers.

The man whistled sharply in a rhythm, and the loose horses veered away from him to come to a standstill by Rowan's spear. Late afternoon sunlight filtered through the trees to highlight the rider as he shot one of the soldiers and fled the glen. *Luska.*

Two soldiers chased after him, fortunately going opposite where Lily had run. The last one slowed, eyes on the spear and horses. Rowan's sword and jacket were a few feet nearer the shore, and the man ignored those.

Rowan dove, and just before the soldier reached for the spear, Rowan leapt from the water and tossed a rock at his mount's rump. It reared, the man grabbed for his sword, and Rowan lunged for his blade. Tucking and rolling, he came up sword raised.

"What is it you want?" he demanded as the soldier steadied his horse.

The soldier, perhaps early twenties with a patchy blond beard, grinned cruelly at him. "We're here to rescue a mermaid princess and return two runaway princes to their kingdom—for a reward."

Tala!

Rowan snorted as he slid his feet to the right, keeping his back to the hopefully friendly forest into which Lily had run. "Since when did arrows come first in that? Or is that a Litvanian specialty?"

The soldier flashed his teeth at him, and his horse surged forward.

CHAPTER 22

R owan leapt to the right, faltering on his weak leg. He caught his spear for support and brought his sword back up, only to be surrounded by the horses Luska had left, them snapping and neighing warnings at their Litvanian brother.

The soldier scoffed as his horse backed away. "You must be one of the princes—animal bonded, are you? You'll be happy to know it's reward before sword for you." He kicked his horse forward.

Luska's horses, by accident or design, forced Rowan back while blocking the soldier's approach. The soldier cursed the horses, and looked about ready to injure them, when something beyond Rowan caught his eye. He turned his horse's head as if to go around. "Ah, I see the ogre. We'll be back for you, prince." He raised a horn slung about his chest, and Rowan threw himself forward. He couldn't let him—

An eagle's angry screech drew their gazes up, and a magnificent golden eagle flew at the soldier's face, claws out. The man toppled from his horse as the eagle slammed into him, slicing his raised arms before nipping his bowstring in two and stealing the sword from his grasp. As the bird kept up its attack, Rowan clobbered the soldier on the head with the hilt of his sword. When the man quit moving, the eagle turned to Rowan and briefly nuzzled his shoulder before hopping back and forth to bring his attention to a note tied to his leg.

Rowan removed the note, and his brother gave a friendly screech and flew away. Footsteps had Rowan pivoting around, sword in hand.

Lily ran from the forest to catch the soldier's shying mount. Two Birney guards he didn't recognize were at her heels, their horses at theirs. Tala, his brave mermaid, was climbing the pool's bank. The loose horses chuffed and stamped impatiently. Each bore a pack and supplies—Tala's, Lily's, and Rowan's among them. He didn't recognize the pack on the fourth horse.

He unfolded Beau's note as Tala ran toward him and the two Birney guards helped Lily onto her horse. The note had only three lines: *Litvania. Will follow. Watch for fiery bird.*

The sounds of a skirmish in their camp rose in intensity, and a suspicion formed in Rowan's mind, but now was the time for flight, not questions.

As if to confirm, their eagle gave a soft cry from within the forest. Rowan caught Tala's outstretched hand, boosted her onto her horse, snatched up the blanket and their shoes, snagged his spear, and the group fled the open glen.

Perhaps knowing the way, or following the eagle's calls, the horse with the unclaimed pack and no rider led them through the forest. Rowan and a guard rode behind him, Tala and Lily next, and the other guard in the rear.

"Where's Max?" Rowan asked a half hour later as they slowed to descend into a narrow gorge. He glanced back at Tala. Though she was wet through and had been riding a horse for less than a fortnight—had been human less than a fortnight—she was handling their journey well. The evening was cold and darkening fast, and he hoped Tala, wrapped in her blanket again, wouldn't get chilled before Beau let them halt to change and dry off.

"On his way to the Golden Tower," Paul, after he'd introduced himself, explained. "Luska is helping clear his path. Litvania's soldiers had already figured out how to get inside before our troops arrived. They've been trying to pick us off from the Tower's windows. We figured the only way to get Prince Max to the Tower courtyard and the bull was if we drew the soldiers out. So Prince Beau and Luska let them know your party was coming. We didn't know exactly when they'd strike, but our guards were ready and joined with yours."

Rowan huffed, somewhat irritated he'd not been included in this planning. How often had Luska and Beau met and he'd not known?

"They left the Tower to hunt Max?" Lily exclaimed from behind him.

"No, or not mostly." Rowan's hand fisted around the reins. "They're after Lady Tala and me as well."

He heard a gasp behind him, but the trail prevented other questions. The horses clopped along the pebble-paved bank of a swift, shallow stream at the gorge bottom.

They'd been forced to light their lanterns, and Rowan was feeling a familiar stretching sensation, when he heard his brother order them to halt in the regal bass voice Rowan had always marveled at and secretly envied. Beau had been born a king, stern, wise, and regal. Max a jester and bringer of laughs, but beneath that a king as well, or would be after a few more years of growing up. Rowan, however, was neither fully one nor the other and a bit more of a creative. Was that enough for Tala? Did the serious mermaid need a joy-bringer? Someone equally serious? Or did, he prayed, she need someone who could be a milder version of both? Someone who could make her laugh yet match her steadiness and understand her creative side?

As the group eased to a halt between a gnarled oak and a prickly holly, Tala pulled her horse alongside his, her leg brushing his in the tight space, and Rowan's heart did a little leap.

Beau, lantern high as he watched them circle around, arched an eyebrow at Rowan. *Didn't she hate you the last time we were human together?* he seemed to say.

Rowan winked, and Beau huffed, a smug smile touching his lips briefly before flattening at Lily's question.

"Why are they after Lady Tala?" She laid a protective hand on her friend's shoulder.

A tingle along Rowan's back had him digging through his pack for the glass bottle and cap, hating that he'd have to leave. Tala was being hunted, Max was facing a deadly bull and soldiers, and he was just supposed to go to sleep as a whale!

"And Rowan and Max, or perhaps the ruby necklace that controlled the sharks." Beau watched with keen eyes but no expression as Rowan slapped the cap onto his head and presented the bottle—the breakable bottle—to Tala. She placed it in her own bag with a care he prayed would one day extend to human him.

"Malosi asked me about having a siren's voice," Tala mouthed, and Lily vocalized, "but that lives only in full sirens. I never had it. I know no other reason he or Litvania would want me. Most scorn sirens and any with siren blood. It is only because of my family's high connections on both sides that any tolerated my mother and me."

Tolerate? How could anyone only *tolerate* someone as wonderful as Tala?

That stretching feeling made even his scalp tingle, and Rowan unclasped his spear from his saddle and held it out to Beau. "I think, having just indirectly helped a mermaid, you can get this to Max. A magical spear for a magical bull seems fitting." *And it's the most I can do for him.*

128

Beau nodded, understanding in his gaze. He took the spear and held the horse's reins as Rowan prepared to dismount. "Siren Voice also refers to the royal line. If he married you, Lady Tala, a descendent of a siren princess, it would give him some claim to the throne, and he wouldn't need to 'degrade himself' by marrying a full siren princess."

Rowan straightened so fast he nearly fell off the horse. *Marry her?* Gathering his thoughts, he managed to dismount without incident.

"If you were looking for a reason to stay human, Tala," Lily muttered, "that's one. Much better options here."

Look at me, Tala. Please look at me.

Beau shifted, Rowan's horse suspiciously sidestepped into him, and Rowan flattened to the forest floor.

Tala looked at him.

So did everyone else.

Rowan grinned brightly at Tala, and the corner of her mouth lifted in amusement before she gave her attention to dismounting. Rowan kicked Beau in the shin, and as his brother hobbled on one leg, he scrambled up, leaves and dirt sticking to his still-damp clothing.

Lady Octavia was going to throw him into the sea for bringing this mess to her shipshape ship, but he needed to speak with her tonight, not just show up as a whale in tow.

"It's time for me to go." He tugged his cap down as the others looked to him in surprise, and Tala, he fancied, with disappointment. "See you in the morning—and save me some breakfast!"

CHAPTER 23

Beau allowed Tala to change and them all to eat, but after that, he set them off again. Litvania was hosting a ball each day for a month, but the month was coming to a close—and they needed to be there to save Meilani and catch that egg-bearing bird that would appear after Max killed the bull.

They traveled into the night, slept hard for a few hours, and woke early. Beau had claimed Rowan's glass bottle for the night, intrigued by the model ship cutting through waves within it, and so after the sun rose, an eagle flew from his tent, then a tousled Rowan emerged, running his fingers through his hair and blinking away sleep.

Tala, seated on a fallen log by the fire, unthinking, scooted over. Rowan smiled at her, gave his hair another good rub, and wandered over to the fire to sit beside her. As everyone greeted him and he them, as conversation flowed again and the guard on breakfast duty dished out their meal, a warmth settled in Tala's chest, a sense of rightness she didn't dare consider too deeply.

They didn't linger over the meal but were soon on the way again, following the path Beau had described. Rather than guide their way, he flew off to get the spear to Max.

That day, they watched the skies as much as their path, hoping for Beau's return and a sight of this fiery bird bearing a burning egg. Around noon, they spotted the golden eagle, a bundle of fabric in its claws. This it dropped at Rowan's feet before swooping away after a hare they'd startled into fleeing its cover. Rowan knelt and unwrapped a horrifyingly familiar outfit from the small pile—a Litvanian soldier's.

The men changed into the uniforms—Tala was grateful no marks of injury marred the fabric—and set out again. A few hours later they left the forest for a worn road. They were within Litvania now, Rowan assured her, but not on a major road leading to the border crossing. They should still be cautious, but it was unlikely they'd be hunted here.

When they came upon a sleepy little village, the guards thought it safe to purchase supplies. It was agreed that Lily, veil on again, would wait in the woods as Rowan and a guard went for supplies. Hardly had the wish to see a human village entered her head before Rowan was towing her along. While the guard purchased food for them and the horses, Tala and Rowan visited shops and peeked into cottages. He bought her a pastry, and as they ate it, they watched children play in the square and an old man strum a lute as a young couple danced.

Far too soon to Tala's mind, they left the pleasant village and all of human life that could be seen there to return to their travels. The afternoon and evening continued as the previous had—a hard ride and another night camping in the woods, for which Beau joined them and Rowan did not.

As she fell asleep, Tala wondered what a human bed with its soft-looking mattress and cozy blankets would feel like on a crisp morning. She imagined it would hold the same stay-put comfort as waking next to a vent of warm water in a snug house of coral and shell.

Another day followed, broken by the sight of a peculiar bird larger than an eagle and fiery red in color flying overhead. Their eagle screeched and took off after it, harassing it and slowing its way. They urged their horses on, following as they could—along the road to Litvania's royal city.

Midafternoon, they halted to water the horses and found themselves blinking against a golden glow, which faded to a halo around Lady Violetta. Back in her violet gown, she held two envelopes in her hand. Tala knew little of human letter writing, but even she guessed these to be formal, costly bits of paper and wax.

"Your invitation to the royal ball, my dear. You're in luck!" she said after greeting them. "Some particular friends of mine, Queen Solstice of New Grimmland and party, are returning from a royal wedding in New Hanschrisland and plan to attend tomorrow night's event. She gave me the tickets for her and Duke and Duchess Houen's daughters, who do not wish to attend. Princess Snow tends to be reclusive." Lady Violetta placed the heavy envelope into Tala's hand, and she was forced to swallow a lump of regret and fear.

She was going with strangers to this ball. She'd have to walk and dance and act like a human. She'd have to find Meilani and convince her to give up the prince and leave, for her kingdom's sake, without a voice.

"Queen Solstice's guards will call for you at the Fiddle and Fox Inn," Lady Violetta continued as Tala wished once again she wasn't going alone. She could ask Beau, but deep down she knew simply having someone wouldn't ease the sense of loneliness she was fearing. Or satisfy the longing for a dance she'd been trying to ignore for days.

Lady Violetta handed her the second envelope, startling her back to the present. What had she missed?

"Who is the second—"

"Just keep it in your pocket, dear. Your gown has pockets, of course, and they won't bulge, no matter what you put in them." She gave Tala a significant look, and Tala drew in a sharp breath.

The story for Meilani—she'd been struggling with figuring out how to get the collection of engraved oyster shells to her at a ball, and here was the answer.

"There's an old fishing shack beneath the cliff on which sits the castle," Lady Violetta continued. "I suggest Princess Lily wait there for you, as her brother will want to see her. Litvania still isn't letting him leave and has forced his betrothed's father into agreeing to allow the wedding to take place in Litvania. She's already on her way. I imagine he'd like a friend to speak with."

"What! Why that—" Lily bit off her words and looked as if she'd like to take the frying pan from their supply sack and whack Litvania's royal family with it.

Lady Violetta nodded seriously. "I agree, dear. Now," she added cheerfully, "don't forget that if the egg hits the ground, it will catch whatever it touches on fire and destroy itself. Prince Max must get it *unharmed* to the mage to end the curse and gain its power."

Tala clasped Lady Violetta's hand in thanks, and the enchantress gave her an understanding smile before hugging Lily and tapping Rowan on the shoulder with a silk fan.

"It's time to be off. We have much to do." She curtsied to Princess Lily and Tala. "We will see you when we see you."

Rowan was leaving? It was barely afternoon! And when was he coming back?

"Keep the bottle in your pocket, Tala, next to the invitation," Lady Violetta warned as a glow built around her and Rowan.

Tala spun toward him, alarm building in her chest. When would she see him again? Was this on business for Birney or for his own family and kingdom, to save it from their step-mother's grasp?

If the latter, would she see him again if all went well with the crystal ball? Would he rush back home? Would she? Someone had to get Meilani back to Crestfall, after all.

Tala found her hand at her throat. It still ached, a little less than at first, but her mermaid body was not healed. Marrying a human prince was of course out of the question. The crystal ball, if it could both heal her body and transform her back . . . yet she didn't want to return to Crestfall without a goodbye from Rowan. And Max, of course.

She stepped forward. "When—"

They vanished, and the guards urged Lily and Tala to their horses.

❧

Lily claimed that human beds varied in desirability. Those in the Fiddle and Fox were good for an inn but did not compare with Lily's at the palace, which, she insisted, Tala must explore as a human. After a short nap on one the next after-noon, Tala was inclined to believe her.

She was not impressed by human baths in portable tubs that maids filled with kettle after kettle of steaming water. Hot springs and warm water vents were far superior, but she was clean, her hair washed, and she hadn't panicked when she'd stepped into the tub.

Tala smiled ruefully as she brushed her hair. Lady Tala of Crestfall could float as a human. She couldn't race the sea horses or play with the dolphin calves, but she wouldn't immediately drown either. And later, when this was done, Rowan could continue her lessons and—

The brush stilled in her hair, tangled emotions rather than knotted strands bringing it to an abrupt and painful halt.

Since when was she more than tolerating her life as a human? Looking forward to it even? She needed to get back to her aunt and uncle, her parents' home, her friends.

Tala tugged on the scale pendant, its chain digging into her neck. Was she meant to live with her aunt and uncle all her life? Hadn't she friends here as well? Memories of her parents to carry with her wherever she was? Purpose in both places?

"Are you okay?" Lily, head cocked, studied Tala, whose brush was unmoving in her hair as she stared at nothing less than two futures.

Tala dipped her chin in response and finished preparing for the ball. Soon though, she was pacing their small chamber, her questions as stuck to her as barnacles. When Lily's concerned look encouraged her to sit, she studied her chain of oyster shells, reminding herself of her kingdom and her responsibilities and history there. But that story always came back to a certain whale rescuing her from the sharks, then braving those same deadly creatures to return a merman home and end their terror. She ran her thumb along the shell depicting a strong and handsome human carrying an injured mermaid to shore.

Rowan.

Even his name declared he belonged to the land. It was the name of a tree that symbolized courage, wisdom, and protection. The name fit him, but it, but he, did not fit the sea.

A heavy weight settled in Tala's chest, where the scale pendant rested, and she returned the shells to her pocket, opposite the one in which she'd carefully tucked Rowan's glass bottle.

Night had claimed the village long before the guards announced a New Grimmland servant. She was soon ushered into a carriage for the first time in her life. Lily followed, veiled. A queen perhaps ten years Tala's senior with a sad, kind sort of smile and a middle-aged couple—a large and friendly man and his rosy-cheeked wife—greeted them as the carriage rolled away.

"We've noticed a rather odd bird in the sky today," Queen Solstice commented. "A golden eagle has been attacking it, or rather nipping at it as if to herd it."

Tala nodded. How long could Beau keep it away from Crystim so Max could capture it and the egg?

Hurry, Max. Be careful.

"I know you cannot speak," Queen Solstice said, her tone sympathetic, "but if there is any way we can help beyond your ticket . . . ?" There was a genuineness to the offer that had Tala studying the trio again. Lady Violetta trusted them, and she'd heard only good of the queen from Lily. She pulled the oyster shell string from her pocket and placed it in Queen Solstice's lap. She tapped her own image before patting her chest.

They studied the shells, and the carriage rolled and bumped its way through the village and into the city proper, betwixt massive gates, over cobblestone streets, and through another gate to a vast palace complex. Litvania was wealthy and liked to show off its affluence, hence a month's worth of balls and an enormous palace.

The carriage left Tala, Queen Solstice, and Duke and Duchess Houen at a set of imposing stairs sure to be worn smooth before morning by the parade of ladies, gentlemen, and servants passing up and down it. Tala prayed all those whose feet were adding to its polish were too consumed by admiration for the grandeur of the building or the clothing of their companions to notice the carriage stop again before the gate and a cloaked figure and two guards descend and disappear into the shadowed paths leading to the cliff beyond the palace.

Grateful for the duke's arm on the crowded, unfamiliar stairs, Tala dared a peek at the sky.

Empty.

Don't let the ballroom be empty of my quarry.

Duke Houen ushered his ladies inside, and they found themselves lost in a flood of humans. To Tala it seemed a kingdom of kingdoms had come for the final week of balls before Litvania "kindly" hosted the wedding of Birney's crown prince to strengthen their relationship. *We'll see about that.*

With the fatherly duke's aid, they pushed their way from room to room and finally to the largest chamber Tala had ever seen. Grander even than her king's great hall, it was lined with windows that glittered in the candlelight and reflected all the colors of the gowns and jewels of the ladies twirling within it. But nowhere did she see Meilani.

She has lavender hair. How hard could it be to find her?

To aid her cause, Duke Houen danced her around the ballroom twice and she accepted the requests of three young men. She had no Rowan counting for her now, giving her a safe and pleasant place to rest her gaze, but Luska had taught her well—and her mermaid grace wasn't all lost—so the dances passed with ease. Though if her partners were offended she didn't look at them, she didn't care. Not with a kingdom at stake. But, alas, the dances were in vain.

No Meilani, not even a cluster of men eager to partner with the pretty mermaid visiting their human halls.

Lysander. Meilani would be with him, trying to win his heart to save herself from sea foam. Lily's brother was a tall, thin man with strawberry blond hair. It was he she should look for, he she could see over the crowd.

She motioned to Duke Houen to dance with her once again, and the kind man, eyes alight with enjoyment of their secret plot, readily obeyed. After one unfruitful pass around the room, they moved from the faster outer ring of dancers to join the slower couples in the center. Meilani was the sort to fly along the floor though, not dawdle, but might Lysander prefer a slower pace? Even Tala loved the feel of the dance as they spun and stepped and moved together as gracefully as any mermaid sped through the water. A dance even with a friend was a thing humans should treasure.

"Any luck, my lady?" Duke Houen whispered as a new song began.

Tala shook her head. There were so many humans here! Yet surely she should be able to spot—

Twirling around the outer ring a half dozen couples up were a pale, thin man with strawberry blond hair and a petite woman with an enviable figure whose raven-black hair had a purple sheen to it. She wore a lavender gown.

CHAPTER 24

Tala stumbled at the recognition of Meilani—and how the transformation had changed her. Duke Houen caught her, and he, with a shrewd glance in the direction she stared, deftly pulled them from among the dancers to a spot where it was safe to be still.

As he questioned her, concern in his tone, Tala fought to overcome her shock. She had been born with human-like brown hair and green eyes, and hadn't thought of anything but her scales and tail at the transformation. But Meilani had been born all mermaid—shades of lavender from hair to eyes to scales. And she'd lost all that as a human. Oh, she was still beautiful, but she wasn't the exotic mermaid she'd likely counted on when risking so much to woo a human.

"That the girl?" Houen asked, then added in a mutter of disappointment, "She's not purple. I was hoping my intuition about that effect of the spell would be wrong. Evie will be disappointed."

Tala nodded, studying both her princess and Birney's prince. Meilani smiled and soundlessly laughed, but there was something forced about it Tala hadn't seen in her before. And there was something worn and tired in Lysander's expression as well. There was nothing hinting at desire for Meilani, alluring though she was. There was tolerance, and perhaps something brotherly. For the sake of Lysander and his betrothed she was glad. But for Meilani . . . Tala prayed again Max could use the crystal ball to uncurse them all.

If Tala had been dancing then, she would have again stopped mid-step. *Am I cursed?* Even though she'd forgiven Rowan, she'd still counted herself among those in need of the crystal ball's aid. But *cursed* wasn't really right for what had happened to her, for her life now.

Unsettled by the question—another form of the one plaguing her since she'd kissed Rowan's cheek—she apologized to Duke Houen with her eyes and let him lead her back to Queen Solstice.

"There's a custom for dancing," he whispered as they neared the wall of those watching the dance or waiting for their chance to join, "that a gentleman can gain another's dance partner by tapping him on the shoulder. Now that we've spotted our quarry, I'll steal her away over here. Perhaps you and Queen Solstice should move closer to one of the doors to the gardens, in case we need to find a quieter place in which to converse."

Queen Solstice gestured to a large open glass door and urged Tala that way as Duke Houen hurried through the dancers to Lysander and Meilani.

"How is this spot, Lady Tala?" Queen Solstice asked with a wave of her fan toward an empty nook between a tall potted plant and the doorway. "The air is less stuffy here with the open door as well. So many candles and so many people do have their effect on the air . . . " She trailed off, her eyes narrowing on something behind Tala.

Surely Meilani wasn't making a scene by refusing the duke!

Tala spun around and found herself staring into familiar eyes as blue and cold as the ocean depths.

Malosi bowed, steady on human legs. Beside him were three men: one bedecked as royalty and two as guards.

Dressed as a nobleman, Malosi's strong human build—and his high position—were evident. Around his neck hung a single pearl as large as her thumbnail and wrapped in golden vines—a common symbol of a fae magical artifact.

"Queen Solstice," he said, his tone as charming in the air as heard through sea water, "this is a pleasant surprise. And Lady Tala, you're looking exceptionally well tonight."

Her eyes snapped to his, a smug tilt to his lips proving she hadn't misheard, that she now knew how he'd managed what he'd claimed so long ago—to have seen a human fireplace without a contraption. Without a curse with a price attached. Somehow, he'd gotten a transformation stone, and heaven only knew what mischief he intended.

"Yes, I still talk. I needed no curse, and paid no price." That arrogant smirk grew before he turned to Queen Solstice, whose narrowed eyes were hinting at a mother's protective anger. Tala gave a slight shake of her head. *Don't do anything to harm yourself. There's still hope he doesn't know we found Meilani.*

The queen of New Grimmland frowned in acknowledgement before smiling tightly at Malosi. "Ambassador Malosi, how good to meet you again. Lady Tala, you should know your ambassador has always been quick to assure us of how hard Crestfall and Litvania work to protect the seas and how grateful we should be for their efforts, especially every time more of New Grimmland's and New Beaumont's ships sink in its waters—and are salvaged by Litvanian crews—than usual off other coasts."

Is that so?

The smirk wavered. "How good of you to remember me, Queen Solstice. The seas are dangerous, but therein lies part of their beauty. Do you not agree, Lady Tala?"

Tala's fist clenched in her skirts, but she only mirrored Solstice's tight smile.

Malosi mocked them both by returning it. "Oh, may I present one of your hosts?" He swept a hand to the side. A hawk-nosed man of about five-and-thirty, with thin lips perpetually in a flat line of displeasure, studied her from beside him. He gave a slight nod of permission to that request to be introduced. "This is Prince Hadrian II, heir to King Hadrian I of Litvania. I am flattered to say he is a good friend of mine."

Queen Solstice and the prince exchanged a slight bow of the head as Tala watched, a blend of anger at this man causing her friends trouble and panic that Duke Houen was going to bring Meilani straight to them. She could see them approaching now, Lysander following. *Not now!*

"Please forgive her, Prince Hadrian," Malosi drawled as the prince's frown deepened. "She is one of mine and doesn't know how to curtsy yet."

His!

A diplomat's politeness intruded on her anger, and Tala considered attempting the act but decided she'd never honor the two men before her. She batted wide eyes instead.

"She dances rather well for such an omission in basic etiquette," Prince Hadrian countered with far too much keenness.

Malosi, a condescending tilt to his lips, merely took her hand in his, as if ready for a dance. A shiver skittered down Tala's spine, but she'd chased a shark once before. She knew to watch her sides now. She wasn't running scared or fighting blind.

"I believe she was taught by a prince of Danskov, Your Highness," Malosi replied, and Tala paled. Who had Malosi among King Basil's men to know that?

Prince Hadrian's lips thinned even more, as did Tala's at that slight to her human.

"Dance with me, Lady Tala?" Not even watching her for a response, Malosi bowed to Queen Solstice and Prince Hadrian and led Tala away. "Such a pity about the voice." He swept her into the outer ring, where the fastest of the dancers flowed with the music, as if they were calling a whirlpool to them. It took all of Tala's focus and skill to match his pace and not trip.

Had he no thought for her ability with her human legs? Or was he testing her? Wanting her to fail? Well, she wasn't going to. Though she might "accidently" step on his feet on occasion.

They flowed around the room with the current, and Tala focused on the challenge of the dance, the beauty of the music, but he, his eyes roamed her face, then down the length of her in a way that boiled her temper. He spun her out and then drew her back in, holding her closer than before. She pushed away, and he chuckled, his gaze raking over her once again in far too possessive a manner.

"You make a passable fair human, Lady Tala. That dress captures your beauty so that you've lost nothing in the trans-formation, unlike poor Meilani. Not even that lavender gown could recapture her lost color."

A knot formed in Tala's stomach, but she raised her chin and glared at him. *I'll knock you upside the head with Rowan's bottle and let him land on you as a whale if you lay a hand on me.*

The muscled bit of detritus laughed. "Ah, so loyal, Lady Tala. Is that what I see in your eyes? Sparking with indigna-tion in a thoroughly enchanting way." His chuckles deepened as a coldness crept into his eyes. He deftly turned them at the end of the room and began moving them toward the slower center.

For that mercy, she nearly cheered. She was growing breathless from the exertion, her throat's ache intensifying. She couldn't maintain either the energy or the focus for such a fast pace. Calling for her attention as well were the murmurs traversing the ballroom of a strange creature flying over the palace—a small dragon or phoenix or fae moth afire.

Hurry, Max. Beau, keep the bird ashore for him!

Malosi, head cocked as if also listening, slowed their steps even more. "You found the foolish guard I clumsily let escape alive and saved him, I heard," he continued. "Do you now think to rescue your princess and so stop King Aleki from surrendering to me? Your pathetic human prince's message may have gotten through, but your uncle can only hold the king back from coming for so long."

Tala felt the blood drain from her face before she set her jaw. Her monarch must think of his kingdom too! And Rowan was not pathetic!

A cruel chuckle declared Malosi had no qualms about using a father's love to enslave a kingdom. "Prince Lysander will never love her, you know. Besides being terribly and honorably in love with his foreign princess, he is fully aware that if he does stoop to pretend to care for her, his betrothed will have an inexplicable accident on her way to their wedding. As for all the other princes about, they've been warned.

"And that crystal ball Prince Maximilian is still chasing, Prince Hadrian hasn't yet taken the bait to go after it, so I'll let it get back to Crystim before I take it. It will not help her either. No, Princess Meilani's time ends the morn after the prince she sought to hook marries another, and Prince Lysander must marry, and soon. Peace depends on it." Sharpened teeth glinted in the candlelight. "And King Aleki will not let his foolish daughter suffer the consequences of her pride. He will come."

"The consequences of listening to her own cousin," Tala snapped, wishing more than ever her words had sound.

Still drinking her in, Malosi slowed their pace and cupped her fingers over his, as if about to kiss her hand. "I rather like you like this, eyes sparking with fury but unable to speak. I will be king of both sea and land, taking the former in one sweep and the latter piece by piece, though Litvania doesn't know it yet. And yet"—he drew her hand toward his lips—"you might be the most delightful conquest of all. A jewel of sea and land."

A sudden sick feeling kicked Tala in the gut. More than disdain or revulsion, it was horror, a deep sense of wrongness such as she'd never felt when faced with an unwanted suitor before. It was the kind of repulsion that only came from a soul-deep certainty of what was *right*.

She jerked back, but he tightened his hold and used his hand under her shoulder to keep her in place.

"Tut tut, Lady Tala." He shook his head, the light of one who loved a fight in his eyes. "Think of how good it would be for your aunt and uncle, how much better for vulnerable little Birney—and Danskov—if they had a powerful man with their good at heart."

She scoffed. *What heart?*

He glanced to the right, where Prince Hadrian and two of his personal guards watched from along the wall. Another guard was approaching Houen as he danced Meilani around the room, talking earnestly to her. "Think of what a scene here could do when you've already refused to honor the prince and sneaked in on another's invitation."

Her knees threatened to give out, frail human things, but Tala again raised her chin.

No.

No. You will not threaten anyone I care for. I will never marry you. We will find the crystal ball and do whatever it takes to stop you.

He studied her face, and she got the feeling he guessed some, if not most, of her thoughts. An arrogant, satisfied smile curved his lips before he brought her knuckles toward his mouth again, and she very much wished she had painted her skin with poison rather than perfumed lotion.

Conscious of the watching prince and guards, Tala steeled herself for the kiss, but Malosi released her hand and turned in irritation to a man repeating a tap to his shoulder.

"May I cut in?" Impeccably dressed in a tailored yet practical suit only a talented enchantress could create, hair freshly trimmed and cheeks attractively shadowed with the start of a beard Tala desperately missed seeing, Rowan grinned at Malosi as if in friendly rivalry. But there was a fire in his eyes Tala had rarely seen.

Her even-tempered Rowan was furious, and it made her deliciously warm inside, or would have if she wasn't terrified the two men sizing one another up would create a scene they couldn't afford.

Perhaps it was confidence in his power, the stern eyes of the watching prince, or the lapel pin she'd not noticed Rowan wearing before—a spear wrapped in patterns of silver and blue, but Malosi released her to Rowan. He stepped away, that predatory, shark-teethed smile flashing, his teeth snapping a wordless threat.

Her human prince merely arched an eyebrow at the uniquely merfolk gesture, glibly thanked him as he pulled her close, and danced her away.

A dozen feet down the line, within the slowest ring of dancers, hidden from Malosi and Prince Hadrian by a cluster of couples, Rowan pulled her into a hug, warm and safe and everything she needed right then.

It lasted far too short a time before he cleared his throat apologetically and resumed a proper dancing hold.

"The plan's not totally scuppered," he said softly, glancing around with the alertness of a nightwatchman. "I fixed it with Lysander to bring Meilani out to a certain garden chamber to meet us, and Houen is describing all your shell sketches to her as they dance. Now we just have to make our own way out without shark boy swimming after."

He glanced at Tala for a response, but she merely nodded,

and he went back to watching and plotting their daring, dancing escape.

Was it shameful all she, a mermaid, wanted at that moment was to press her cheek against a human's chest and listen to his heart beat, let the touch of his lips to her fingers wash away the horror, the wrongness, of a merman's?

A slight hitch to the dance brought Tala's thoughts back to the ballroom. Rowan didn't dance as smoothly as Luska or even Malosi, as fluidly as she'd imagined, and she had imagined it far more than she was willing to admit. She'd seen him swim and fight, though, when danger made all else forgotten, and so knew his prowess. There was a tightness about his eyes now suggesting pain, and Tala suspected his injuries, aggravated by that swim and fight, and followed by hard riding, made each step a punishment.

And yet here he was.

He'd gotten the timing of his transformation switched back so he could be here with her. He'd come to her rescue when it pained him, and when it exposed him to the men who'd sent soldiers to capture him. And all this after she'd been unkind to him for days, after she'd declared she intended to return to the sea.

Aside from a fit of panic that had saved her life, from the day she'd met him, he'd been wise and kind, virtuous and strong, a dependable friend who shared many of her passions and who made her laugh. Who was willing to sacrifice for her. Who was willing to not only fight for her and with her, but for his own dreams and plans as well.

A heart like his wasn't met with every day, in land or sea. The question was, should she catch it or throw it back?

Rowan slowed them to a walk and placed her beside him, her arm through his. "I think a visit to the refreshment table, then the garden is in order. That merman thinks he's a hawk, the way he watches us."

Hawk . . . Bird. What if Max caught the fiery bird and got

the crystal ball to the mage before seeing them again? He was going to use it to heal her and change her back. She wasn't ready yet! She needed more time with Rowan to know.

Heart pounding with urgency, Tala tugged on Rowan's arm until he looked down at her. His gaze darted away to a guard near the wall behind the refreshment table they were approaching before settling on her, reminding her of their danger. "Yes, Tala?" He brought her hand to his chest, his thumb softly stroking her skin. The motion drew her eyes to the spear pin. He'd seen Max then, or Beau had seen them both. *Good.* She needed him, someone with a voice, to get to Max.

Tala brought her other hand up to wrap around his. "Rowan, don't let—" *Max change me back yet.*

"Rowan of Danskov." Music ceased, dancers stilled, chatter died as a voice like a hurricane swept through the room. "You are under arrest for the theft of a magical cap belonging to Lady Porsche of Mage Isle, wife of the king of Danskov."

CHAPTER 25

Tala gasped. Under arrest?

"Fish hooks," Rowan spat, and then he darted for the refreshment table, dragging her along beside him. A guard who'd been stationed near the door rushed him. Rowan tossed a punch bowl in his face; caught the stumbling, splattered man; and slung him into the soldier coming from behind. They overturned a table and fled between table legs and wall until coming to a doorway half blocked by a servant with a tray of champagne flutes. He stumbled and glasses clinked as they scrambled past.

"Sorry!" Rowan called out as they dodged more servants carrying trays of various delicacies. One bearing an empty tray came from a doorway to the right, with stairs visible beyond. Rowan pulled her into the dark stairwell, his pace not slacking. She'd only taken stairs thrice before—at the inn that day and outside the palace—and never at a run! But she couldn't remind Rowan now.

"Keep hold of my shoulder. Tap me if you're having trouble," he called back, and Tala couldn't stop a smile. The best prince in all the world was currently on the run as a common criminal.

Though was there anything common about a human able to steal a mermaid's heart?

While Tala prayed for stamina for her human legs, guards crashed through the kitchen above, shouting questions. Footsteps pounded after them, sure and confident human ones.

"Rowan." She tugged on his sleeve until he glanced over his shoulder. "I'm fine on the stairs, but that cap we're being chased over?"

"Only good for one travel a day." He gave her hand a squeeze and ripped the pin from his lapel. The spear appeared in his hand. They ran from corridor to corridor, slammed doors while running past to mislead, hid a hair's breadth from sword-wielding guards, knocked others off their feet with one swipe of the spear butt, backtracked and double-backed, until they seemed to have traversed the entire palace. When they burst back into the ballroom, Tala was too breathless to laugh, or weep, at where Rowan had led them. Instead, she remembered her own purpose.

Houen was ushering his wife and Queen Solstice out under the watchful eye of the palace guards. Lysander and Meilani were nowhere to be seen—again. The chatter of the royals and nobles floating just above the music was a blend of tales of a fiery bird, fleeing lovers, and cunning thieves.

"Good heavens! There they are! Catch them!"

"Help the poor couple, you heartless fools!" Houen's booming voice rang through the chamber. "This is nothing more than a plot to separate them!"

Guards and dancers crushed together, some straining forward and others stoutly blocking their way.

Rowan, limping now, guided her through an open glass doorway onto a garden terrace. He wove them between couples watching a golden eagle drive a fiery bird from the shore and the sailboat waiting in the harbor. With a last look at the birds, they plunged into the garden maze, peering into each chamber and walkway they passed. Though some were occupied, none held their friends. *Please let us find Meilani and Lysander! Please let us find them! Please—*

"Wait!"

A lean man leapt from behind a curtain of ivy in the shadows of a chamber they'd thought empty, and Rowan and Tala ran back to join him. From behind the prince stepped a young woman, graceful and lovely.

There was little beyond moonlight and a few lanterns in this part of the garden, but there was enough light for Tala to see human Meilani studying her and Rowan.

It wasn't a proud and selfish princess taking her measure, calculating what cost she could exact to get her way. It was a little girl, scared and alone and for the first time in her life, feeling the cost of her choices.

Though part of her wanted to blame Meilani for what she'd done and what it might still cost, Tala opened her arms instead, and Meilani rushed into them.

"Will you agree to leave?" Tala asked and Rowan voiced. "I think—" *Max can help you too with the crystal ball, since it was Crystim you made the pact with. We'll keep you from sea foam somehow.*

Meilani's head nodded against her shoulder, and Tala froze. Meilani pulled back to look her in the eye and again nodded. *No buts, I'll go*, she seemed to say. Meilani peeked at Lysander and briefly hung her head. *I was wrong*, Tala heard her heart say. Lysander gave Meilani a sad, but proud smile.

"Princess Meilani understands the harm it would cause not only to my betrothed," Lysander whispered, "but to the relationship of our kingdoms, to so many people, if I married her. Malosi, that—" He bit off his words and continued in a calmer tone. "He tried to get her to stab me so I couldn't marry—and she'd never turn to sea foam—but she refused. She's chosen to honor her agreement, come what may. She's asking for you to send word to her father that this is her wish, that he fight for his kingdom and let her act honorably."

Tala turned to her princess, shock, pride, and sorrow warring in her chest. Meilani nodded, so solemn and unlike the girl Tala had watched grow up.

"I will fight for my kingdom too, in the only way I can now," the princess mouthed, and Rowan vocalized.

Tala pulled her back into a hug, squeezing her tight. *You are a princess and a mermaid to be proud of.* Barely had Meilani's thin arms wrapped around her again when avian screeches, human curses, and loud footsteps echoed through the gardens.

"I don't care who that eagle really is, stop it. The fiery bird must get to Crystim in the harbor," Malosi shouted. "And find the mermaid and that prince who dares flaunt a merking's weapon. Bring them to me."

CHAPTER 26

"Go. Get to the fisherman's hut. Lady Octavia is sending a longboat for you." Rowan, gripping the spear in one hand, pushed the girls toward the arched chamber doorway, but Lysander caught Tala's shoulder and pivoted her toward the opposite end of the chamber. Nearly hidden by ivy was a narrow wooden door.

"That way." He hurried past her to shove it open and lead the way through. Grabbing Meilani's hand, Tala followed and found herself not in another garden chamber but at the corner of a broad terrace ending at a cliff. A few partygoers milled about near the railing, watching the enigma of an eagle trying to shepherd a fiery red bird of a type they'd never seen.

"This way." Lysander took Meilani's other hand and urged them toward an unassuming gate near the palace walls to their right. "This will take us to the shore and the fisherman's hut."

Beyond the gate, a stone-paved stairway descended steeply toward the water. There was no shore, Tala gathered, immediately below the fenced terrace. It was water crashing into a rocky cliff base. But this winding stair journeyed to a pebbled beach and a ramshackle hut.

As Lysander and Meilani raced through the gate and down the stairs ahead of her, Tala very much wished for Rowan's hand on the steep, damp, and dirty path rather than slight Meilani's. Tala glanced back over her shoulder, but Rowan wasn't there.

"Do you think, human," Malosi's voice echoed angrily in the salty wind, and Tala's heart lurched, "that by laying that spear you stole down that I cannot pass to claim what is mine?"

Yours? Indignation and purpose pumping through her veins, Tala slipped her hand from Meilani's. Her princess glanced back, but Tala shook her head, shooed her forward, and ran back up the stairs.

"I think," Rowan said, "that you could walk over it—but you cannot lift it."

Tala pled with her burning calves and burning thighs to move faster. Malosi wanted her alive. She wasn't so sure about Rowan. A bowstring twanged, and several ladies cried out.

They were shooting at Beau! There had to be some way she could stop this! She *would* stop this. And she would tell Rowan she'd made her choice.

"You dare challenge me? A cousin to the merking?"

"A traitor to the merking."

Tala dared lift her gaze from the rock paving stones to the gate, over which she could see Rowan's head and shoulders, then all of him.

"Get out of the way," Malosi snarled, his hand hovering near the blade at his waist, "or we'll sell your blubber to the whalers sooner rather than later."

"Pick it up and I'll move, shark boy. If you can."

Tala, chest heaving, came to a sudden standstill on the

second step from the gate. Crouched and sword drawn, Rowan blocked the pathway, standing a few feet within the terrace. Three paces before him, between him and Malosi—and a dozen soldiers and Prince Hadrian—lay the spear in a type of merfolk challenge Tala had no idea Rowan knew. An unexpected weight tugged at her pockets, and she withdrew her stone dagger. She'd stabbed a few dangerous sea creatures with it. Mayhap she'd get the chance for one more.

Gripping the handle, Tala crept to the gate. Malosi watched, arrogance turning to something else—a blend of fury and, surprisingly, hurt—as she met his eye and touched the flat of the blade to her forearm and kissed her fingers to Rowan. *I give my strength to my loved ones.* She flicked the blade toward Malosi. *My teeth to their enemies.*

Turning from her, he spat at Rowan, "Perhaps you should direct your efforts to keeping your feathered brother alive."

In response, two arrows whistled through the air, and an eagle screeched and flapped wildly before regaining its composure. The fiery bird darted past toward the sailboat, which now drifted near the harbor exit, beyond the hut.

"No!" Tala screamed and ran up the final step. They had to get that crystal ball for Lily, for Rowan and Beau and Meilani.

The men who'd not seen her before jerked her way at her movement. Malosi and Rowan both lunged for the spear. Malosi reached it first but couldn't lift it, for he was a traitor to his kind. Rowan snatched it up, twisting and slamming it into Malosi's shoulder, barely missing his head.

Screams and cries of anger burst from all around, blending with the whistling of a longbow's arrows, the whack of Rowan's spear and Malosi's blade, the incongruous clatter of horses' hooves over marble flooring, and the shriek of a magical bird.

An arrow meant for the eagle hit Crystim's creation. It

exploded in a cascade of burning feathers and a flaming ball that dropped on the fisherman's hut. It burst into flames as Malosi cursed that the ball would be ruined.

Lily. Lily and her guards were in that collapsing hut. Meilani and Lysander were on their way if not already there.

"Lily!" Tala couldn't even scream her fear. Someone yanked her away from the gate into the terrace as six stallions as black as night thundered out the palace ballroom and across the terrace, toward the gate. Luska rode point, two of his horses following beside him, two behind, all neighing and kicking, clearing the way like some unstoppable ebony wave. Within their circle, riding low over his own dark steed, was Max.

They drove the archers from their spots, broke bows under their hooves, scattered guards, and sent Malosi diving from their path. Just before the gate, they broke and turned, some to the right and some to the left. Max rode straight, leapt the gate, and flew down the path, his body thrown back against the horse's rump as they plunged onward toward the hut and Lily and the possibly shattered crystal ball they'd all placed their hope in.

"Tala, the glass bottle!" Rowan spun Tala toward him, yelling over the chaos as Luska's horses surrounded them, driving Prince Hadrian's men back. "Give me the bottle!"

Fearing the reason, Tala tugged the glass bottle with the model ship from her pocket. She couldn't let him leave thinking she still wanted Max to set her free from her "curse." That was the last thing she wanted! Begging Rowan to stay still long enough to see her words, she held out the bottle and met his eyes. "Rowan, I want to sta—"

Rowan pulled her into his chest, kissed her, tugged the bottle from her limp fingers, and plunged into the melee. Slamming the into the polished stone flooring, he sprinted between horses and soldiers and partygoers, eyes set on the terrace railing. He leapt onto it and launched himself into the air.

It was a blue whale that crashed into the sea, creating waves that rocked the waiting sailboat and flooded the shore, briefly swallowing a burning hut. Steam hissed and billowed into the air. Three men and two women clung to one another and the rocks as water surged and retreated around them and a black horse and its rider flew past to the remains of the hut.

"Stop him! Do something with your men! He mustn't get that ball to Crystim." Malosi, yelling at Prince Hadrian, darted toward the railing himself, the fae pearl artifact glowing.

Tala slapped the rump of the nearest horse, and it charged forward, sending Malosi veering from his path. At a whistle from Luska, another horse herded him from the railing as Tala sprinted toward him with all her human speed. Malosi ducked another horse, backed up, and crouched to spring for the railing and waves. What chaos he could cause she didn't know, and she was determined not to find out.

Coming in from an angle, she threw herself at him as he launched himself out. One hand closed around the pearl and the other around the railing. He plunged toward the sea, and she tipped with him, desperately clinging to both railing and pendant. The necklace snapped, as did her grip on the railing. Malosi cursed and fell, his legs turned to fins, and for a moment, Tala feared she was going to follow.

Gentle hands caught her and tugged her back, steadying her as her feet found purchase. The pendant warmed in her hand, and visions teased her mind and heart. Visions of Crestfall, of sea canyons and open oceans crossed with ease, of sapphire blue scales and a tail whole and sleek. Of human legs dancing, climbing mountains, and walking beside kings and princes.

For a moment, time stilled. *This is what I need.* Held within her hands was the answer to everything for her. Healed body or not, this magic could turn her human to mermaid and back at will. She could marry Rowan and not lose anything.

"That isn't what you think, Lady Tala." Luska stood at her side, a weary expression on his face. He lifted an open palm toward the pendant. "Nothing from the fae ever is."

Tala's fingers closed protectively over it. The pendant was lovely in itself, and the power it gave . . . *No cost*, as Malosi said.

Or was that true?

The fae lied and cheated. Is that what she would be doing if she took this and married Rowan? Would keeping a foot in both worlds truly be choosing him?

Some things, like an immortal soul, were too costly. Only one greater could pay for it to save those he loved. But some costs should be paid, or consequences accepted, by those who owed them.

Did she, like Meilani, need to accept the consequences, good and bad, of her choice to love Rowan? To truly choose to marry a human, she had to choose to be human and accept all the costs that came with it. Her mind and heart both said this was where she was meant to be. They also warned there was a wrongness to the pendant, that forcing a way to what she wanted through it might succeed and yet still fail in ways she couldn't see now.

Why do you always think of Rowan, as life as a human, with its friendships and opportunities, in terms of cost paid and not treasure gained? Like a miser who regretted everything she spent money on.

No, she wouldn't view Rowan and all her life as a human as something she'd unwillingly sacrificed for, bitterly regretting all she'd lost for it. It would be a treasure she paid a great price for out of love. She wouldn't deny the price, but she wouldn't regret it, not for the treasure she'd gain.

Face already turned to the gate down to the cove, Tala

dropped the necklace into Luska's hand. He lifted her onto a horse and sent them racing down to the pebbled beach, where her friends were climbing aboard a longboat, soon to row into the harbor, where a beautiful blue whale was blocking a sailboat's attempt to sail away from the rightful end of a bargain.

CHAPTER 27

Rowan had to admit to thoroughly enjoying using his large snout and tail to play with Crystim's tiny sailboat. The sorcerer squealed like a little girl as he clung to the mast while his crew fled in a lifeboat. Rowan let them leave but kept up his antics on the weakened mage, not letting him alone long enough to try any magic on him or on the boat cutting through the waves toward them, Tala on board.

He let that thought sink in. She was safe, and she wasn't running away.

If she slapped him for kissing her as soon as he turned human, he'd understand, but he'd needed to let her know he wanted her to stay before she got to Max and his little brother fixed Rowan's impulsive plea to a soft-hearted enchantress.

As the longboat neared and Crystim spotted Lady Octavia's head gunner, he ceased his squealing and gave an enormous sigh. Playing done, Rowan swam carefully away to not risk any waves tipping his friends into the water as they boarded. Nor did he want to hazard dislodging the eagle sitting beside Tala, her examining a wound on one wing.

Max, Lily, and Gerron boarded Crystim's sailboat, Max carrying the crystal ball bundled in his fireproof jacket. Lily's clothes were covered in ash, and she coughed on occasion, but she seemed unharmed as she took Max's arm and faced the mercenary who'd made her hideous and whose scheme had cost at least one prince his life. Mostly she just looked dripping wet and mad.

Soft movements of water behind him had Rowan turning and rolling on his side to see who'd entered the harbor. He was of a mind to ram any Litvanian vessels, but this one was of shadows and moonlight on waves. Few mortal men would ever see Lady Octavia's ship without her permission. Before it though, safe and sound, was a royal vessel from the kingdom of Lysander's betrothed. Water rippled before both ships, and a pod of merfolk swam to the surface. Tala's aunt and uncle, a solemn king with a crown of coral and pearl, guards, and several others floated in the waves. Held within a cluster of four strong guards was Malosi. Hands bound, he writhed and snapped his teeth, but the guards held fast, and they soon disappeared under the waves. Rowan rolled until his eye was under the water and he saw them swimming away toward Crestfall.

Wondering if whales could smirk, he rolled back over until his enormous eyes were again above the water. He gave a kind of wave to Lady Octavia, then, like her, he watched and waited. Soon, there was a ripple in the air that skimmed along his back, tingling the magic of his curse.

Lily was free.

Now, Max and Gerron had to reclaim the crystal ball from an unwilling sorcerer. Fear churned in his very large gut. Then it was freedom for him and his brothers. Meilani, he hoped. And Tala . . .

Ask her again, Max. Things have changed since that night she cried on your shoulder. I know they ha—

Another ripple flowed over him, a sensation of shrinking

he knew all too well, and yet there was something different about it this time. It felt permanent.

Rowan, a tall human again, splashed into the sea, and Lysander cried out in victory.

But by the time Rowan heaved himself into the boat beside a human Beau, a pall seemed to have fallen over everyone. Everyone was staring at Meilani. She held herself still and calm, shoulders proud. Only her tight grip on Tala's hand gave away her fear.

At a sob, Rowan looked to the sailboat. Max and Lily, who was now stunningly beautiful despite tears shimmering in her eyes, stood on the deck, a cracked crystal ball in Max's hands.

The sorcerer had lied about how much power the crystal ball—he, himself—possessed, and it was far, far less than anyone thought.

Rowan settled quietly into his seat, and Meilani turned to him with a smile. Rising, she gestured for him to take her seat beside Tala. She pointed to the bow, where the merfolk king waited.

The guards seated there moved away to give her privacy with her father, and Rowan hesitantly sat beside Tala, studying her studying him. Was she disappointed she was stuck in human form? Relieved? If so, did he have any part of that?

When her face gave nothing away, he sighed and ran his fingers through his hair. It was a lot to ask, and—

Something dropped into his hand as it rested on his knee.

Tala's scale pendant, the one she so often looked at with longing.

His eyes snapped to hers, and she smiled timidly. Then his mermaid wrapped her arms around his waist and pressed her cheek against his wet chest. Though too shocked to speak, he wasn't too shocked to wrap his arms about her in return. Her arms tightened, holding him as closely as she'd once held that pendant.

"I guess we're stuck with each other, huh?" he teased softly when he could find his voice.

He expected her to nod, but she raised her head instead, shook it, and returned to her position against his chest, snuggling in as if it was where she *wanted* to be. Where she'd intended to be all along, crystal ball or no.

Rowan, I want to sta—

Stay.

That's what she'd been trying to say earlier, when in his haste and fear he'd interrupted her.

Smiling like a fool, Rowan hugged her back and kissed her hair. "Stuck together in a different way then, huh?"

This time, she nodded.

⚜

The next week passed swiftly. The wedding Litvania had been attempting to host by force was moved to Birney. Litvania withdrew its soldiers from Birney's borders and generally ceased its rumblings of conquests and sinking ships. The sirens fell silent, their waters calm, and Crestfall's visitors to Birney reported seeing a shadowy ship near their kingdom. No one saw Luska after that night at the palace, and Rowan wondered what larger plans the man had, but whatever he was up to, he'd helped them not to further his cause alone, Rowan believed, but because he believed it was right.

When Lady Violetta arrived in a violet haze to check on her fairy goddaughter the night her curse was removed, she suggested the case of the stolen cap be brought up to Mage Isle, along with the ruby necklace and the question of how Crystim had known where to find Lady Octavia. Three days later, Rowan's stepmother agreed to an annulment and

163

transferred fairy godparentship of the three princes to Lady Violetta. As much as he liked Lady Violetta, Rowan would have preferred Lady Octavia, but his former step-aunt refused to have anything to do with Mage Isle.

And there was still the matter of the sea foam curse she'd written and whose extreme terms had been so blithely accepted.

🐚🦋🐚

Meilani danced at Lysander's wedding. Bright and joyous as others watched, sorrowful yet not despairing or bitter when she thought they weren't. What Lysander and his bride said to her, Tala did not know. She only knew that before leaving for their wedding trip, Lysander kissed Meilani on the forehead and his wife, teary-eyed, hugged her tightly.

Tala, Rowan, Lily, and Max spent that night with Meilani in the grotto under Birney's castle, pretending they were ordinary friends celebrating one wedding and planning two more. Near dawn, Meilani's father and grandmother and Tala's aunt and uncle came. Meilani smiled at them, more at peace than Tala had ever seen her. As dawn kissed the waves, she walked out to the beach and into the sea. The waves crashed into her, knocking her under and foaming up.

Lily clapped a hand to her mouth to stifle a cry, and Tala squeezed Rowan's hand and bit her lip.

The waves rolled back, leaving a long and slender lump of lavender scales and lavender hair. The lump twitched and moved and disappeared under the waves again.

Once again the waves retreated. The lump was gone, only foam in its place.

Unable to bear any more, Tala started to turn away.

"Look!" Lifting Tala's hand in his, Rowan pointed to a boulder rising from the waves a half dozen feet from where Meilani had disappeared. Thin arms clutched the rock and slowly pulled a young mermaid from the sea. Foam covered her tip to tail, the bubbles swiftly popping in the cool morning air. With them dissolved Meilani's hair and the lustrous coating of her scales. A sudden wind blew the rest away with the finality of a captain giving command.

Meilani, bald with dull scales, looked at her tail and felt her smooth head. She clasped a hand to her mouth, but laughter still escaped. She met Tala's eye, as if to confirm the truth she was alive, and when Tala nodded, grinning, Meilani threw herself into the water and into her father's arms.

"She's lost her beauty. That was the death?" Rowan's tone was both incredulous and grateful. He glanced over his shoulder.

Surprised, Tala followed his gaze, and for the first time noticed a form in the shadows of the cliff face behind them.

Reluctantly it seemed, Lady Octavia strode from them, surprisingly lovely in Lady Violetta's lady sailor ensemble. Despite the improvement of her looks, the feared Queen-Guard of the Sea sighed. "I told you I wrote the spell during a dark period in my life. I wanted to kill what I saw as pride and cause shame. I never intended for it to be used again. In a year or so, she'll be just as beautiful as before."

"No," Tala said with a sniffle, "she'll be more beautiful."

Rowan handed her a handkerchief. "But still not as beautiful as my mermaid."

EPILOGUE

I t was a year before Tala regained her voice. Her first words were, "I love you, Rowan." Shortly after, she said, "I do," in a small ceremony on a pier, where those she loved best from her two worlds could see her wed a human prince. Following that, Meilani and her aunt and uncle braved the contraptions to join her and her husband in the castle for a much grander ceremony for Lily and Max.

The contraptions, Lily had gleefully announced after Tala had accepted Rowan's proposal, were his childhood handiwork.

I was twelve years old, he'd protested when she'd given him a piece of her mind, mostly for the fun of it. *My father thought the artwork was hilarious and that King Basil would simply repaint them. And I would have loved your feedback to improve them!*

Your father, Lily explained, *didn't count on the fact that my grandfather and Tala's uncle were also once twelve-year-old boys. They love seeing Tala's and Aunt Tiare's indignant glares at the contraptions every time they see them.*

When Rowan caught Tala smiling and shaking her head

at the contraption with the octopus being stepped on, he leaned close and whispered, "I can repaint those, you know."

Enjoying his closeness, Tala shook her head, then, as she often did these days, reminded herself she could speak. "Leave them, as a reminder to not take life too seriously, and never by appearances." *Not as I once mistook you as a cruel fool and life as a human as unbearable.*

Rowan smiled gratefully. "That is wise advice, wife, in general, but there is one very important area by which I shall take it by appearances."

Tala cocked an eyebrow at him. "What's that?"

Chuckling, he lifted their intertwined fingers to his lips and kissed her wedding band. "By that smile and the light in your eyes, by how comfortable you look leaning against me, I'd say you were a happily married woman."

And you'd be right.

৩৵ঌ

A year later, on a sunny afternoon as Tala painted a landscape of Crestfall for Max and Lily's rooms at the palace, she heard a horse approach the cottage she and Rowan lived in while in Birney. As ambassadors for the merfolk for Birney, Danskov, and Litvania, they often traveled between the kingdoms. Tala loved Danskov, with its mountains, forests, and rocky cliffs, and treasured their home there, but her garden and sandy seashore in Birney held her heart just a touch tighter.

A dog's bark followed the clatter of hooves up the cottage lane. Not expecting anyone until Rowan returned at dinner —with her promised anniversary present—Tala walked to the window. An older couple rode up the path, the woman clinging to the man she sat behind for dear life. She wore a gown of iridescent turquoise stitched with silver and he a suit coat of the same over brown trousers. They were both riding astride, polished leather boots visible.

Dropping her paint brush, Tala ran from the cottage, calling to two of the most wonderful people she'd ever known, and two of the last she thought to see on horseback and here.

"Tala!" her aunt cried as she clung tighter to her husband, the space between them barely large enough for the kitten there. "Tala, how do we get off this monster? However did you manage to ride for days? My two legs are more than enough, but this creature has four!"

"Oh bosh, dear. You get off in reverse of the way you got on, of course," her uncle replied, the thrill of adventure lighting his entire face. "It's as easy as falling off a log, as we humans say."

"We don't say that," Aunt Tiare squealed. Tala skidded to a halt and spun away, searching for a bench or bucket to aid them in dismounting. Hugs would have to wait until they were safe aground.

As she attempted to gather her thoughts—scattered between joy and wonder and question—into the practical matter of getting her aunt and uncle down safely, she vaguely noted the kitten meowing, the hound bounding around investigating the shrubbery, and a carriage rolling to a halt in the drive. From the latter peered a dearly familiar face, a mischievous grin making it all the more handsome. Her husband held up a folded stepladder.

Tala stilled her frantic searching as Rowan stepped from the carriage and tossed her a wink. "I see your anniversary gift made it safe."

Tala's mouth fell open, and she glanced between Rowan and her aunt and uncle.

"I hope you have rooms ready, my dear." Smiling as broadly as a little boy up to mischief, Uncle Fetu held out his hand. "Lady Octavia assured us it would be hard to undo this 'curse.'"

"He wanted his horse and his dog and his cat." Aunt Tiare huffed fondly as Tala hurried over to grasp her uncle's hand. She claimed Tala's free hand for herself. "But I wanted time with my dear Tala and my grandchildren whenever they come."

"And Lady Octavia wanted to make me happy." Rowan set the ladder beside the horse and slipped an arm around Tala's waist. "Which generally involves making Tala happy, and so here we are."

"All happy and all home." Tala smiled as the hound leaned against her useful, not-too-unattractive-when-you-were-used-to-them human legs.

ABOUT THE AUTHOR

E.J. KITCHENS loves tales of romance, adventure, and happily-ever-afters and strives to write such tales herself. When she's not thinking about dashing heroes or editing her own and others' books, or teaching about writing, she's enjoying the beautiful outdoors or talking about classic books and black-and-white movies. She is a member of Realm Makers and lives in Alabama.

May she beg a favor of you? You've already kindly read her book, would you also leave a review? Those gold stars can power more than fictional worlds: they encourage, inspire, and help authors through hurdles so we can seek out the people looking for books like ours to read. It's a daunting quest, and without you, fearless reader, it would fail. Would you join it?

To learn more about E.J. Kitchens and her books, editing, and writing course, and to receive a free short story, visit her website and sign up for her newsletter:

www.ejkitchens.com

OTHER STORIES FROM THE INTERTWINED TALES

The Intertwined Tales is a multi-author series of clean fairy tale retellings. Each novella entwines a famous fairy tale with a lesser-known story to create one happily ever after.

❧❧❧

THE MERMAID AND THE CURSED PRINCE is also part of E.J. Kitchens's Curse Keeper, Curse Breaker fairytale series.